Helen's heart spe

He hadn't said a word about her outfit, but she'd seen the quick flick of his eyes over her, the way he had quickly lowered them to guard his reaction, and sexual tension had sizzled through her like a live electric charge.

This was all new to her. Life had always been so well organised. This...? She could write off a silly crush, and she could almost shut the lid on those stolen moments between them, when things had got out of hand, because thankfully they had come to their senses. She could very nearly blame it all on being in a bubble, back there in that ridiculously romantic hotel where barriers had been blurred just for a moment.

But now Helen was agonisingly aware that the sand was shifting ever more beneath her feet.

She knew the kind of guy her boss was and she knew that it would be fatal to let herself get sucked into his magnetic orbit.

Secrets of the Billionaires' Secretaries

Unbuttoned by the off-limits boss...

Behind every man there's a great woman.
And behind Gabriel and Malik are their skillful
secretaries, Helen and Lucy. They not only keep
Gabriel's and Malik's non-stop schedules in check,
but the billionaires themselves!

But whilst Helen's and Lucy's abilities to put the
playboys in their place is unquestioned, their
newfound attraction to their bosses has them
questioning *everything*...

When Helen is mistaken as Gabriel's fiancée, they
are forced to maintain the wedding charade, in
order to clinch a vital business deal!

A Wedding Negotiation with Her Boss

Available now!

And an unexpected return to Malik's kingdom leads
Lucy to a promotion at the royal altar...

You won't want to miss Lucy and Malik's story

Coming soon!

A Wedding Negotiation with Her Boss

CATHY WILLIAMS

HARLEQUIN

PRESENTS

ISBN-13: 978-1-335-59344-3

A Wedding Negotiation with Her Boss

Copyright © 2024 by Cathy Williams

Recycling programs
for this product may
not exist in your area.

For questions and comments about the quality of this book,
please contact us at CustomerService@Harlequin.com.

TM and ® are trademarks of Harlequin Enterprises ULC.

Harlequin Enterprises ULC
22 Adelaide St. West, 41st Floor
Toronto, Ontario M5H 4E3, Canada
www.Harlequin.com

Printed in Lithuania

MIX
Paper | Supporting
responsible forestry
FSC® C021394

Cathy Williams can remember reading Harlequin books as a teenager, and now that she is writing them, she remains an avid fan. For her, there is nothing like creating romantic stories and engaging plots, and each and every book is a new adventure. Cathy lives in London, and her three daughters—Charlotte, Olivia and Emma—have always been, and continue to be, the greatest inspirations in her life.

Books by Cathy Williams

Harlequin Presents

Desert King's Surprise Love-Child
Consequences of Their Wedding Charade
Hired by the Forbidden Italian
Bound by a Nine-Month Confession
A Week with the Forbidden Greek
The Housekeeper's Invitation to Italy
The Italian's Innocent Cinderella
Unveiled as the Italian's Bride
Bound by Her Baby Revelation

Visit the Author Profile page
at Harlequin.com for more titles.

CHAPTER ONE

'TELL ME I haven't caught you sleeping...'

Helen Brooks sat up, blinked at the telly—which appeared to have changed programme from the detective series she'd been watching to something about over-sized mansions in LA—and cleared her throat.

'Of course you haven't!'

It was Saturday. It was a little past nine-thirty and, yes, she might not have been *sleeping* but she'd definitely been *dozing*. More to the point, why was her boss calling her at a little after nine-thirty on a Saturday night?

He read her mind. 'Because it's only nine-thirty UK time, if I'm right. Shouldn't you be out and about, now that I think about it?'

Helen heard the amusement in Gabriel's voice and she could picture him without any trouble at all—unfairly sexy, black eyes framed with lush lashes most women would have killed for and a body that was all muscle and sinful perfection. She had been working for him for a little over three years and she knew, just *knew*, that her uneventful life was a source of constant amusement for a guy who never stood still.

He played hard, worked harder and seemed to thrive on no sleep at all. When he wasn't working, he was having fun with sexy blondes who all seemed to run to type. And she should know, because she'd met a number of them over the course of time: pocket-sized, big-breasted, breathlessly seductive and, it always seemed, eager to please. It annoyed her just how much time she wasted thinking about her boss and his ever-changing parade of girlfriends. Frankly, it annoyed her just how much time she wasted thinking about the man in general.

'That's right,' she said. 'And how can I help you?'

'That's very formal, isn't it?'

'Gabriel, why are you calling me on a weekend when you're in California and should be… Wait, what time is it over there?'

'About one p.m.'

'Why are you calling me on a Saturday evening?'

'It's work-related, I'm afraid.'

Helen was instantly alert. When it came to work, he could count on her, although wasn't he supposed to be taking a vital one-week break before the work began?

'It's Saturday, Gabriel. Surely anything to do with work can wait until after the weekend?' She hesitated. 'And, um, I thought you were there with… I forget her name…'

'Fifi.'

'Oh, yes, of course—Fifi.' Fifi, whose real name was a more pedestrian Fiona, had been on the scene for a little over four months. Helen had sent flowers to her twice, arranged multiple dates for Gabriel and her at the theatre and various fancy restaurants, had supervised the purchase of an extremely expensive bracelet and had physically met her once a few weeks earlier when she had shown up, unannounced, at the eye-wateringly beautiful offices in the City that housed Gabriel's UK headquarters.

Fifi was small and busty with a tangle of bright-blonde

curls that fell to her waist and which had been artfully scooped up in a ponytail on the day she had showed up in a very tight keep-fit outfit. This was, she had explained in a high, breathless voice, because she'd just come from the gym and thought it would be nice to go for lunch somewhere with Gabriel if he wasn't busy.

'Weren't you having some long-overdue time off relaxing with… Fifi…before you met Arturio? I'm sure that's what you told me.'

'That was the plan.'

'I don't suppose she'll be impressed that you're on the phone to your secretary on a Saturday to discuss work,' Helen pointed out.

She muted the volume on the telly and curled into the sofa. Somewhere deep inside, she was conscious of feeling a little guilty and a little exasperated with herself that the sound of his disembodied voice down the end of the line made her feel like this.

She was twenty-eight years old. Perhaps she should have been doing something more adventurous, something *more fun* than watching telly after a vegetarian pasta dinner for one, but she had never been into clubs and bars, and she had never seen the point of forcing herself to take an interest in them simply because she happened to be in London. She had a small circle of girlfriends and she occasionally went out for meals or to the theatre or cinema with one of them. If she chose to stay put on a Saturday evening, she wasn't going to beat herself up about it. A quiet life growing up in Cornwall had set a path for her that she wasn't ashamed to follow.

Until her boss's amused voice got under her skin and made her think again. Outside, the setting sun had left behind a pale-grey sky streaked with watercolour-orange.

It was still summer-balmy and through the windows she could hear the laughter and voices of people passing by, people out there having the sort of fun she, annoyingly, now felt she should be having.

She absently played with her ring finger, brushing the spot an engagement ring had once encircled, and pushed aside those intrusive thoughts.

'Hard to tell because she's not here.'

'But I booked her into the same hotel as you. Did I get the flights wrong? I'm sure I booked her on a first-class flight to get in the day after you arrived, which should have been two days ago!'

'Calm down, Helen. You did and she arrived.'

'Then I don't understand…'

'Long story. No, scratch that—really short story. Suffice to say that things didn't work out between us and she stormed out earlier this morning.'

'Ah.'

'Am I reading judgement behind that "ah"?'

'Not at all. I'm sorry things didn't go according to plan, Gabriel. But I still don't understand what that has to do with anything.'

Judgement?

Helen would never have gone beyond her brief to tell her boss exactly what she thought of his attention span when it came to women, because it was none of her business; but, yes, there had certainly been judgement behind her softly uttered, monosyllabic comment on what he had said.

She had no idea why women were so helpless when it came to him, because take away the crazy good looks and the over-the-top generosity and, at the end of the day, what they were left with was a rich guy who couldn't commit and didn't have to.

A little voice whispered that that one-dimensional picture certainly didn't do him justice, but Helen was adept when it came to swerving away from the disturbing notion that she knew all too well what women saw in her sinfully gorgeous and charismatic boss.

Easier to stick to the basics, and the basics remained that, in all the time she had worked for him, she couldn't remember any relationship lasting longer than a handful of months. Between these relationships, there would be pauses but never for that long.

He had form. Surely those women knew him for what he was? He was like a toddler with an attention span of five minutes when it came to relationships. It wasn't as if he didn't make frequent appearances in the glossies at some event or other with a woman on his arm, smiling up at him with adoring eyes. There was ample pictorial evidence on record of a guy who didn't have staying power, so why bother to go there?

He represented the very last sort of man on earth she would ever allow herself to get emotionally involved with, whatever his looks, charm and bank balance. Irritatingly, it just beggared belief that her body sometimes refused to play ball with what her head told her, so that the mere thought of him could set up a chain reaction inside her than had her nerves jangling.

Such as now. She surfaced to hear him saying something about an accident and she immediately asked him to repeat what he'd just said. Her pulses quickened and she straightened, all meandering thoughts put to one side.

'Thought I'd hit the gym when she flounced out and seems one of the weights I decided to tackle was a little too adventurous. Picked it up and managed to twist my hand in the process.'

'You *twisted your hand*?'

'It's shocking, I know, but I'm only human after all.'

'That's awful. Are you in pain?'

'Thank you for the concern. It was nicely bandaged by an attractive redhead and nothing stronger than Paracetamol called for, you'll be relieved to know.'

'You don't seem too distraught that Fifi has left, if you don't mind my saying.'

'I don't mind, and I'm not, as it happens.'

She heard his momentary hesitation down the end of the line and wondered whether he was tempted to tell her what had happened.

He never had in the past. Relationships came and went and she usually found out when the flowers were being sent to a different name at a different address.

Cut to the chase—what he got up to was his business. They couldn't have been more compatible when it came to work. It sometimes felt as though they could interact on the work front without saying anything at all. That said, forays into her private life were not encouraged, and that was something she had been firm in pointing out from the very moment she'd joined the company and started working for him.

Yes, he knew the basics. He knew where she'd been born, where she'd studied for her qualifications and knew the nuts and bolts of the academic journey that had led her to his towering offices in the City. Everything he knew about her he had gleaned from the impressive CV she had produced for her interview over three years ago.

But her private life? Of that, he knew nothing.

He knew absolutely nothing about the guy to whom

she had once been engaged. He knew nothing about how perfect she had thought George Brooks was for her, the perfect guy for a girl who had been conditioned by her background to avoid the risky unpredictability of the fast lane, who had learned to prize safety and stability. She'd been to school with him and had dated him from the age of seventeen. All their friends, not to mention his parents and her dad, had seen their marriage as a foregone conclusion. In the little town in Cornwall, where everyone had known everyone else, theirs had been the fairy-tale romance—just without the fairy-tale ending.

It had been for the best—she'd told herself that a thousand times. If things hadn't been right for him, then the marriage would have come unstuck sooner or later. And he had been right: right to break up before vows had been exchanged; right to follow his heart, which had taken him straight into the arms of another woman within months of their break-up; and he had been so gentle when he had let her down, careful with his words and concerned for her well-being.

And yet, to be ditched was to question one's own worth, wasn't it?

She had moved past that miserable time, had weathered the well-intentioned, cloying sympathy of friends, had removed herself for life in London and had taken valuable lessons with her.

She'd toughened up. When it came to guys, she had built a wall around herself because she never wanted to be hurt again. Her past, her wounded heart and her insecurities when it came to men, would never be open to public scrutiny, least of all by her boss who would never understand where she was coming from.

She thought now about Gabriel breaching that unspoken divide between them and letting her into his personal life. She decided, with a suddenly fast-beating heart, that that was something she didn't want because there was no way she'd ever want to be tempted to return the favour.

They were worlds apart when it came to their views on relationships and she felt painfully vulnerable at the thought of her confident, sexy boss having any insight into what made her tick. There were boundaries in place between them and she liked it that way. She always had. Her right to privacy was non-negotiable, because if any cracks appeared there then who knew where that might lead? And, deep inside, she knew that there was a dark, unsettling awareness of him as a man that could prove way too threatening if it was ever allowed oxygen.

'So you've called me because…?' Back to work, back to familiar terrain.

Gabriel's voice softened. 'Arturio is in the vicinity, as it happens. Decided to come earlier with his wife for a little holiday and wanted to check out the vineyard himself to see whether the grapes would complement his own high-quality product. As you know, for him the sanctity of the Diaz label has to be preserved.'

Helen smiled. It was something she and Gabriel had discussed when the deal to take over Arturio's vineyards in Tuscany—a worthy addition to Gabriel's in California— had first been mooted well over a year ago.

Although Gabriel was based in London, and always had been, his roots were in California, and many years ago some of the vast fortune left to him when his parents had died had been invested in a vineyard that had drifted into neglect over the years.

Gabriel had hired the right people to do the right things, thrown money at the venture and then had decided to go further just as soon as his Californian grapes were doing their thing. He'd told her he'd decided that drinking good wine was not nearly as satisfying as watching how good wine got made, and he had promptly scouted around for an Italian vineyard, a reconnection with the country both his parents had left behind.

He had found more than he had expected. Casual at first, his hunt had led him to a family connection that had lain buried for years. Arturio, as it turned out, was connected to Gabriel's family on his grandfather's side, and establishing that connection had been the cement to Gabriel taking over which would otherwise probably never have got off the ground.

Arturio's high-quality vineyards were perfect, and over the months Gabriel had become more and more personally involved in their acquisition. Reading between the lines, Helen had worked out that he had immersed himself in something that represented a link to a past he had never explored, or even known about, and it had grown into such significance that even she was anxious that nothing jeopardise the final closing of the deal.

'Worked well, what with Fifi leaving,' Gabriel was saying down the end of the line. 'I'm not sure she would have appreciated having to be side-lined. Of course, Arturio was full of apologies about arriving ahead of schedule, but it worked well, getting my guys to give him a guided tour of the vineyard before he signs off on this deal. And I'll admit, I like having him here, like showing him that he has nothing to fear when it comes to selling to me. Means a lot that he enjoys the idea of everything being kept in the family.

'I'll get to the point. I've brought the whole thing forward by a week now that Fifi has returned to the UK and I need you here.'

'But you were going to manage the whole business yourself!'

'When it was just a case of preliminary steps, but it seems Arturio is keen for a conclusion. Wants to get on with the business of happy retirement. He's well over seventy, after all. Who can blame him? Personally, I can't think of anything worse than retiring, but he tells me that he has enough kids and grandkids to keep him busy for the next hundred years. At any rate, there's going to be a hell of a lot more detailed work to be done once the all-clear is given and I'll need you to be on hand with that. Aside from which, there's a limit to how much I can do with my right hand strapped up for the next couple of days. I'm capable of a lot but I still haven't got to grips with ambidexterity.'

'Me come to California?'

'You come to California. Is there a problem with that?'

'Well, not as such…'

'You *do* have a passport, don't you?'

'Of course. Yes.'

'And it *is* up to date, I take it?'

'I suppose so, yes. Of course.'

'Splendid. I'll want you over in time for us to go through the nuts and bolts of this deal. Tomorrow would work.'

'Tomorrow?'

'Helen, why am I detecting a certain amount of hesitancy? You'll be here for three or four days max. I've already assembled my legal people and, whilst it still has to be finalised, I don't anticipate any last-minute hitches. It should just be a case of sitting in on a few meetings and taking minutes.' He paused. 'Late notice, I know, but I'm really not seeing what the issue is. This is important. Dogs and men will have to be rearranged for a few days. Where's the problem in that?'

'Dogs and men?' Helen parroted faintly.

'Can't account for any other obstacles to your getting on a plane and coming over here which, I don't have to remind you, is all part and parcel of a job that pays very well indeed.'

'I realise that, Gabriel,' Helen said stiffly.

There was no question that she was paid well over the odds. In the space of three years, she had had several pay rises, not to mention two very generous bonuses. It was his way of making sure she didn't defect. She wasn't indispensable, because no one ever was, but she was pretty close to being that.

From everything she'd heard from friends and colleagues she worked alongside, his longest serving PA had been a middle-aged lady who had been with him for donkeys' years until she had decided to up sticks and move to Australia to be closer to her only daughter and her grandchildren. After her had come a series of 'unfortunate events', as Karis in Accounts had drily told her a few weeks after she'd joined. Girls who hadn't been able to function at all in his presence, who became nervous and tongue-tied the minute he was around them, who developed girly crushes on him and then proceeded to show up for work in ever more inappropriate clothes.

For all his colourful and ever-changing love life, he was deadly serious when it came to work, and Helen knew that he would do whatever it took not to jeopardise the relationship with the one person with whom he worked so well.

Hence the fact that he was always happy to accommodate her wherever he could. But there were limits, and she realised that she was butting against those limits now. He wanted her there, and there had been steel in that mildly spoken remark about her duties and her healthy pay cheque.

'No dogs,' she said quickly.

'And men?'

'That's none of your business,' Helen returned coolly, because it *wasn't*, and she heard him laugh softly under his breath. She couldn't remember if he had ever asked her directly about her private life. Had he? Maybe he'd thrown out one or two general questions about what she'd done over the weekend, now and again, but never about men. He had a vibrant and energetic sex life. Had he ever stopped to wonder about hers? Or did he think that she had none, that she stayed in every evening while the world turned around her?

It gave her goose bumps to think of her sexy boss speculating on her private life; it made her wonder what it might feel like if their worlds collided and if those dark, lazy eyes turned in her direction and saw her as a woman instead of just his trusted employee. Would her need to be safe be blown to smithereens? If she were ever to trust a guy again, it certainly wouldn't be a commitment-phobe like Gabriel. And yet there were times when she looked at him from under her lashes and felt the force of his compelling, powerful sex appeal trying to suffocate her resolve.

'Of course it isn't.'

'You may not mind the world knowing what you get up to with women, but some of us are a little more circumspect when it comes to things like that.'

There was a telling pause down the end of the line and

Helen could have kicked herself for falling into the trap of saying too much.

'I... I'll let you know what flight I've booked.' She rushed into speech to cover up her discomfort and to paper over the awkward silence that had greeted her impulsive little outburst. 'It may not be possible to find anything at such short notice.'

'It won't be a problem, Helen. There are always available seats in first. You know where I'm staying. Probably the most convenient thing would be to book yourself into the same hotel, and feel free to go for the most expensive suite on offer. I wouldn't want you to be uncomfortable while you're over here.'

Because she'd kicked up a fuss about going in the first place, much to his bewilderment? Because she was paid a small fortune and going abroad on business was all part of 'the generous package'?

Had there been sarcasm in that remark he'd made?

Helen was a creature of routine, someone who liked being in her comfort zone. He wasn't to know that, of course. He wasn't to know that the circumstances of her life had made her the person she was now, and that stepping out of that box always seemed to take so much courage, even when she knew that those steps were tiny and insignificant.

Things would have been different for her, but she had lost her mother and brother long ago in a car crash. She'd barely been eight when it had happened, and it had been a big deal. She had read about it long afterwards, scouring the newspaper clippings about the tragedy on the M4 when a lorry had jack-knifed, causing multiple crashes and twelve fatalities.

In the aftermath, her father had become a changed

man. She could vaguely remember someone more relaxed, someone laid back and carefree, but those were distant memories, overtaken by the reality of a dad who, having lost his wife and son, had become so terrified of losing his daughter that he'd wrapped her up in cotton wool and taught her the value of never taking chances.

'Stay safe and take no risks': that applied to everything, from the emotional to the physical, and Helen, who absolutely adored her father, would never have dreamt of going against the grain.

She'd studied hard, skipped school trips abroad—because who knew what could happen on those ski slopes?—and had never been out too late when it came to teenage parties, because she couldn't be sure that drink and drugs might be going to feature.

When she and George had become an item, her father couldn't have been happier. George had been a known quantity, destined to become an accountant, to work in the nearest town and to look after Helen in the way her father had felt she should be looked after.

Looking back, she could see that she had been seduced by the notion of a safe future over and above everything else. She'd been too young to appreciate that there was a lot more to a for-ever relationship than feeling safe within it. She'd been in love with the idea of being in love, and only in hindsight did she see that there had been a lot missing from their relationship; that, although 'safe' was a good thing, there really was such a thing as 'too safe'.

Leaving to work in London—her one big adventure—had been her only deviation from everything she had absorbed over the years and she still smiled when she thought back to her dad's reaction to her decision. Even now, he remained fond of warning her about anything and everything that could be found lurking down mysterious dark alleys and behind corners. But, disillusioned and desperate to see a different world out there, staying in Cornwall and finding work at the one of the local offices had been inconceivable. She had dug her heels in, and in fairness, although her dad had raised the usual worried concerns, he had caved in without too much of a fight. He'd understood that she had to do that for herself, for her recovery.

Her relationship with Gabriel obeyed all the laws she had laid down. She kept her distance. She worked hard, was extremely clever when it came to IT and could arrange his life with absolute ease, but never had the line between them been crossed.

She felt comfortable within that boundary. This was the first time a trip abroad for business had happened. Largely, when he went abroad, he handled things himself. The business with his hand, combined with the acceleration of this vineyard deal with Arturio, had skewered that, and she could hardly blame him for expecting her to go out to pick up the slack.

Yet the prospect of interacting with him beyond the office confines in London was oddly intimidating.

Nuts. Why should it be? They would still be working, even if the scenery would be different.

'Of course.'

'We have everything online but make sure you bring the physical files as well. Arturio has only recently stepped foot into the dawning of a new century. He delegates, but over here he'll be flying solo, and he might want to flick through the paperwork.'

'It's nice that he's old-fashioned like that.' Helen half-smiled and thought of her dad, who was the same, even though he was much younger. He used to work as a scaffolder but, now that he was retired, he had taken up his lifelong passion for fishing, and dabbled in some lucrative fishing for Cornish crab, which he sold to some of the restaurants in the area. What use had he ever had for IT skills? Perhaps his curiosity had died when his family had been lost to him and he had never bothered to breathe it back into life.

'Nice but time-consuming,' Gabriel remarked with wry, affectionate indulgence. 'Having to go through everything with pieces of paper and written reports. That said, I'm fond enough of him to indulge him in however many paper files he wants us to provide him with. I had no idea you were fond of the basics, considering you're the smartest person I know when it comes to everything to do with tech.'

Helen blushed and was relieved he couldn't see the hectic colour in her cheeks.

'His love for tradition goes beyond the superficial stuff of wanting everything in hard copy,' Gabriel continued into the silence.

'What do you mean?'

'He's a family man. You've met him a couple of times—you can see that straightaway. He carries an album of pictures of his kids and his grandchildren on him, in his briefcase—showed them to me the last time we met—and I must say there's something a little unfamiliar about seeing the faces of people whose blood I share. I know more names of sons and daughters and their many and varied offspring than I would ever have imagined possible when I first thought about scouting around for a vineyard I could buy close to the place my parents were born.

'It's a blessing that Fifi decided to cut short her stay

here, to be perfectly honest. I have a feeling Arturio would have been a little disconcerted by her if they had happened to meet. He's laid it on thick about the importance of family and preserving the tradition within the company, and I suspect Fifi might not have played into that mindset.'

'But you're single,' Helen said, astonished. 'What does that have to do with the deal?'

'Nothing at all,' Gabriel drawled. 'He is the way he is, and this is a fledgling family bond I don't want to risk losing, never mind the tangible practicality of what I'm buying.' He laughed softly and mused under his breath, 'There's a part of me that thinks that the bond with Arturio and his family might actually trump the dry, financial business of buying his vineyard. If he chooses to think that I'm built along the lines of his own children— who all seem to have bought into the joy of weddings quickly followed by the pitter-patter of tiny feet—then I would hate to disappoint him.'

'Well, I'm sure he'll be pleased with its success when you take charge,' Helen said vaguely, nimbly steering the conversation away from anything personal, although she was aware of the faint buzz of curiosity inside her.

Why had his hot blonde decided to leave? Surely a different country, beautiful scenery, the end word in luxury and having one hundred per cent of Gabriel for the better part of a week would have been conducive to keeping her glued to the spot? Had they had some kind of argument because Arturio had shown up unexpectedly and Gabriel had tried to side-line the blonde? That would not have gone down well. From what Helen had seen, she didn't think that Fifi was the kind of woman who would take kindly to maintaining a low profile to accommodate Gabriel and a business deal.

'I'll email you the details of my flight, shall I? Although there's no need for you to change any plans you may have made for the day. I can easily find my own way to the hotel and contact you once I'm there.'

'I'll ensure a driver is waiting for you.' Helen heard his soft, amused laugh down the line once again and gritted her teeth.

'Perfect. I'll see you in due course. Goodbye.' And she disconnected the call before he could say anything further to unsettle her.

Helen had booked the hotel for Gabriel and Fifi without paying a scrap of attention to the details. She had been given the name of the place, had called it and had reserved the most expensive room. Fifi had done the sourcing of the place and Gabriel had acquiesced without demur. The eye-watering price of the room would not have raised an eyebrow.

She could have checked out the place herself now, and had vaguely planned to, but at the back of her mind she'd associated Fifi with somewhere incredibly expensive and incredibly busy, a place where she could bask in the admiring glances of people around her. She'd ended up way too busy to bother checking out where she would be heading to.

She had a smooth trip over—made all the more seamlessly comfortable because, as a first-class passenger, she had actually been able to sleep because the seat had reclined into a bed. Helen only felt a twinge of curiosity about where she was going when she was ensconced in the chauffeur-driven limo Gabriel had organised for her. All glass, perhaps? A skyscraper with uniformed guards outside and the frantic bustle of millionaires entering and leaving? All of the above?

She had never been to America in her life and, as she gazed through the tinted windows of the long, black limo, she felt transported into another world entirely, so different was it from London, from Cornwall—from every destination she had ever been to.

The skies were a milky cornflower-blue and the sun streamed down like honey on a drive that skirted a stretch of coast with water as turquoise and as still as a giant lake. The Pacific coast, the driver explained, glancing at her in the mirror. He was obviously proud of his city. He pointed to the drama of the mountains that rose in majestic peaks behind the town, explained that Santa Barbara was referred to as 'the American Riviera' because of the gorgeous weather and boasted that the beaches were the best in the country, as were the restaurants and cafés that lined them.

There were no frantic, gridlocked roads, just beautiful winding little streets with picturesque boutiques and wine bars, and there was greenery everywhere, showing her that she'd never be far from nature in this part of America.

'I'll have to make sure to take a day off to explore,' Helen said politely, although she had no intention of doing any such thing, because this wasn't going to be a sightseeing, tourist's holiday.

She was busily scouring the skyline for the modern, glassy and expensive skyscraper she'd been expecting and was disconcerted when it failed to materialise.

Instead, the tour-guide conversation from her driver turned to the beauty of the foothills of Santa Barbara. 'Open space,' he boasted proudly, taking one hand off the wheel to make a sweeping gesture encompassing the scenery they were now passing, 'With brilliant views of the oceans and the mountains and a playground for all sorts of incredible wildlife. Hawks, coyotes, a thousand different species of birds, and of course the exclusive real-estate reflects the demand for a place like this.

'And where I'm taking you…' he threw in as an aside, 'Couldn't be more secluded…'

'I beg your pardon?'

'It's incredible. Could never afford to stay at a place like that myself, but my, I've driven a couple of people out there—and, well, if I win the lottery that'll be number one on my go-to list.'

'Secluded? *Secluded?* It's a *hotel.*' Secluded was not what she'd expected, because somehow secluded was something she associated with 'laid back' and laid back was the last thing Fifi was. Had she been remiss in not doing some due diligence before she'd headed over? Or had she been so wrapped up thinking about her boss in a different setting that practicality had taken a back seat?

'Sure, ma'm, but it's a hotel with a difference.'

'What do you mean?'

'You'll see! You'll find it's a bit different from your London, ma'm. Although, you have your royal family, and that's the next thing I'll do with my winnings! A trip to that palace of yours to see those guards with the big, furry hats! My wife would love nothing more…'

Helen was barely listening. She'd expected something big, modern, expensive and impersonal—part of a chain of five-star hotels, something stuck in the middle of the city, in the heart of the action, surrounded by night life, and noisy with the bustle of tourists.

With dismay, she discovered that she couldn't have been more off-target in her assumptions. There were no city lights where they were heading. Instead, the limo slowed in surroundings which, in the fading light, seemed to be a wondrous panorama of landscaped acres interrupted by towering sycamore trees, and fragrant with the smell of citrus and olive groves.

She rolled down her window and breathed in the aroma of blossoms, jasmine and magnolia. Everything told her that Fifi had done her homework.

She'd turned her back on what Helen would have expected and gone for out of the ordinary. No impersonal, height-of-luxury, five-star hotel but...*a ranch*? Or something that looked like a ranch. Definitely not a hotel along the lines that she'd been expecting.

Her heart flipped and dropped.

Her driver had mentioned the adjective 'secluded' and he hadn't been lying. This place was tucked away. It nestled into the greenery and was part of the magnificent landscape, and there was nothing built around it as far as the eye could see.

'Secluded' didn't come close. This was more than secluded. This was...*romantic*.

'Here we are.'

'This is the entrance?'

'I'll help you with your bag.'

'It's okay. It's not terribly heavy. I can manage.'

'No trouble.'

Her bag looked ridiculously out of place here, Helen thought as she stepped out into the balmy evening air.

There was just a hint of a cooling breeze, carrying with it the fragrant smells that had wafted into the car. But they were more intensified, sweet and aromatic, now that she was hovering outside the brightly lit reception area. To one side, a young couple walked past into the night, murmuring in low voices.

Blinking, she turned to retrieve her bag, which the driver had hoisted out of the car. He laughed and shook his head and then, when she spun back round, there he was—her charismatic boss. Framed in the doorway, hands shoved into the pockets of his trousers, looking every inch the drop-dead gorgeous billionaire that he was.

But this drop-dead gorgeous billionaire wasn't in his dark suit, white shirt and hand-made shoes. This drop-dead gorgeous billionaire wasn't attached to his laptop, firing out instructions and attired for work. He was attired for fun and frolics. He was wearing a white short-sleeved polo shirt, cream chinos and a pair of tan loafers.

Breathing in deeply, Helen walked towards him while behind the driver followed with her minuscule pull-along into which she had crammed sufficient work clothes for three days.

'You're here.'

'Where else would I be?' She stopped to look up at him, taking in the rakish stubble on his chin, and thinking that none of this was what she'd had in mind when she'd booked her plane ticket. Not the rakish stubble, not the casual gear and not the romantic setting.

The polo shirt stretched taut across broad shoulders. When she tore her eyes away from the breadth of his chest, they collided with the length of his muscular legs encased in those cream chinos, the easy grace of a hard, sinewy body that was shockingly attractive because it wasn't sheathed in work attire. She felt faint.

'Who knows?' Gabriel drawled with amusement. 'After all the umming and ahhing, it did cross my mind that you might just find an excuse to wriggle out of coming.'

'I wouldn't have dreamt of it.' Helen cleared her throat, eyes skittering away from his suffocating physicality. 'As you pointed out, I'm here to work. It's what I'm paid to do.'

Gabriel's lips twitched.

'Of course you are.' He stood back, allowing her to brush past him into the foyer of what was, in essence, a one-storey, uber-luxurious cottage surrounded by all manner of plants, flowers and foliage. The only indication that it wasn't someone's house was the marble reception area and the two cheerful young girls manning it. 'How could I forget that when you're here in your work clothes, ready and eager to send emails and read reports, even though you've just spent over ten hours on a plane?'

To which there was no answer, Helen thought.

This banter... She had strayed beyond her comfort zone, and she grappled with sudden unease, but he was smiling and she returned the smile, because it was late, she was tired and tomorrow was another day. Things would be back into perspective tomorrow. Work would be on the agenda. This crazily sexy guy would conveniently be back in his box.

But somewhere deep inside her a little thread of nervous tension began to unfurl. She had to remind herself that the professional hat she wore, the one she had been at pains to keep firmly in place, was far too secure ever to be dislodged just because familiar signposts had temporarily been removed.

CHAPTER TWO

GABRIEL FOLLOWED HER through and took charge at the reception desk.

'Nice passport picture,' he murmured, holding it up for scrutiny before handing it over to the girl manning the sleek marble desk, and then grinned at her stony expression. 'How was the trip here?'

'Very comfortable, thank you.'

'Good.' He eyed her outfit, standing back while the young woman at the desk blushed and went through the usual check-in stuff, her eyes studiously averted from him. 'Why are you dressed for work? Surely you didn't expect me to greet you with a list of things to do? I believe in a hard day's work but I'm not that much of a task master.'

Yet had he expected anything different? Gabriel had never seen his dutiful, hard-working, talented and exceptionally self-contained secretary in anything other than formal clothes: suits, white blouses and neat jackets, all in a range of colours that reminded him in no uncertain terms that life was serious business and the work arena was no place for frivolity. Strangely, they had always made him wonder what she and frivolity might look like if they were ever to come up close and personal.

She was a little over five-six, with brown hair that

dropped in a shiny, straight curtain to her shoulders, although in fairness most of the time that shiny curtain of hair was pinned back. She was slender, with wide-set brown eyes, a neat little nose that tilted just the tiniest bit and a little sprinkling of freckles across the bridge of her nose that made him think that she burned in the sun.

He dated sexy, voluptuous women, women who enjoyed displaying their assets, and yet he had always thought that there was something curiously compelling about his quiet, serious little sparrow with her clear, smooth skin, her considered conversation and her unexpectedly husky voice.

'I'm not dressed for work.'

Gabriel pushed away from the marble desk, told Pammy, the woman at Reception, that he would deliver his guest to her quarters and retrieved the pull-along from the ground, tut-tutting when Helen tried to take it off him and point out the fact that his hand was bandaged.

'My other hand is in fine working order,' he told her. 'So there's no need for you to worry on my behalf. If that's what you were doing.' He grinned and changed the subject. 'There's a nice pool here. You should try it. Relax a little, and don't tell me that you're not paid to relax.'

'Okay, then, I won't. This isn't quite what I was expecting.'

'No?'

Walking alongside her, Gabriel felt some of his edginess dissipate. The time-out holiday with his now departed ex couldn't have gone less according to plan. Instead of fun and frolics, he had found himself in the eye of a hurricane almost before the last item of clothing had been unpacked from her Louis Vuitton suitcase—one of three he had bought for her because she'd wanted to travel in style.

She had stepped out of the very same limo that had just delivered his secretary and looked around her with an expression of satisfaction. Something in her purposeful stride had warned him that all was not going to be smooth sailing.

That said, he had not been prepared for the sudden upping of the ante in their relationship, which she had brought to the table without any warning before romance had had much of a chance to blossom.

She had wound her arms around him, breathed huskily into his ear, drawn his attention to the extraordinary romance of their setting—which had made him think that she had chosen the venue for that very reason—and whispered that it was time to take their relationship to the next level. At which point, things had gone downhill at speed.

Gabriel shoved that to the back of his mind and slowed his pace as he ushered Helen out through the landscaped grounds to where she would be staying.

'I expected something more conventional,' she admitted.

'When you say "conventional"…?'

'A big hotel,' Helen confessed. 'Somewhere a little more in the thick of things. I didn't see the need to look up the place before I arrived.' And that was what came of jumping to all sorts of false conclusions…

'I was a little surprised myself by what I found when I got here.'

'Didn't you discuss the choice with…er… Fifi?'

'She said it was going to be a surprise and I was more than happy to leave it at that.' He shrugged and swung a sharp right under a little avenue of trees with branches charmingly entwined to form a canopy. They emerged into a delightful clearing in which a handful of beautiful little cottages was spread against a picture-perfect landscape of climbing plants, mature trees and scattered benches. Each cottage had a porch and was fronted by three broad steps.

'Here we are.' He nodded to another of the cottages. 'Mine's that one. Slightly bigger but no more luxurious.'

'I'm in a cottage…'

'And behind this little cluster of cottages is the swimming pool, although you'd never guess that it was man-made. They've done a great job of blending it into the backdrop.'

He swiped a card and nudged open the door with his shoulder, stepping back to let her pass.

The space was far from impersonal. Helen stepped through into a front room that was adorned with a range of artefacts and artwork that spanned the continents, from a bold abstract painting on the wall above the stone fireplace, to a series of exquisite African sculptures ranged along the window ledge.

She turned full circle and stared. The wooden floor was warmed with faded Persian rugs and through an open doorway she could make out a grand four-poster bed with requisite canopy and soft net drapes that fell to the floor in a swirl.

'Wow.'

'All the cottages have their own small private plunge-pool—added seclusion. Step outside and you can enjoy breakfast brought to you sitting on the veranda at the back which overlooks hillside gardens.' He laughed. 'I'm beginning to sound like a tour guide. Frankly, I thought about switching to something in the city centre, but in the end I didn't think it was worth the effort.'

He watched as she strolled off to inspect the rest of

the cottage. She dumped her handbag on the sofa, along with the jacket she had been wearing, and tucked her hair neatly behind her ears.

Eyes on her as he leaned against the wall, Gabriel absently reflected that she was the only woman who was happy to ignore him, and in that extremely polite way of hers was never afraid to tell him exactly what she thought. It was curiously appealing. The less she said, the more he wanted to know.

She might not offer opinions on his love life, but did she really imagine that he didn't know exactly what she thought of it? She had just the right turn of phrase when it came to revealing her thoughts without actually having to be blunt. She kept herself to herself, and made sure never to encourage curiosity, yet he recognised that curiosity was never far away when he thought about her.

She was still young, yet he had never got even the passing impression that away from the office she was doing all the stuff most girls her age did. Had she had her heart broken? Was she still clinging to lost love, stuck in a moment in time and unable to move on? Never in the slightest curious about the women he dated, he could never resist letting his imagination wander when it came to his secretary.

'Is it going to be convenient doing business…er…here?'

'Come again?'

'You know what I mean.' Helen raised her eyebrows and stood in the middle of the room, hands on her waist. She nodded at her surroundings. 'Is there a conference room on the grounds, for instance? If lawyers and accountants have to gather, where are they going to do that?'

Sensible questions and yet, looking at her as she stood in front of him, the very essence of matter-of-fact practicality, he couldn't resist lowering his eyes to say with a contrived frown, 'I think it could work very well, having everyone here in these pleasant, informal settings. My cottage is bigger than this. There's a very useful table that seats six. As an alternative, we could always choose to discuss the details by the pool...have drinks and food brought to us. The restaurant here comes with an excellent reputation.'

His lips twitched as she stiffened and he burst out laughing. 'Relax, Helen. I have suitable arrangements in place at one of the hotels in the city which is close and convenient. I also have a timetable, you'll be pleased to know. Tomorrow, meetings are lined up with the lawyers. Day after, we consult with the finance guys. Day after that, we can run through the finer details, after which you are free to leave. I will see Arturio on my own to explain what's in place and work through any further concerns he might have regarding the rights of all his employees— all the business stuff that's quite separate from everything else. Especially considering a fair few of them are related to him.

'Everything is in writing and pored over at length, but my gut feeling is it's something that will be raised again, and I want to make sure signatures are all in place before I return to London. So, formalities will be strictly observed, rest assured. Although...you'll have ample free time to practise your swimming in the pool. There's no need be shy about that.'

Looking at him, Helen suddenly felt the ground shift ever so slightly beneath her feet.

Of course he was gently teasing her about everything being in place work-wise, just as he had gently teased her about the formal clothes she had opted to wear for the trip over. Why on earth was she so uptight about a little bit of banter? It wasn't the first time he'd smiled and said something he knew was mischievous, knowing that it would get under her skin. So why was she unsettled now? Was it the change of scenery? She was going to be here for three days, after which she would head back to London and, as he'd made clear, their days would be accounted for.

So, relaxing around a swimming pool? Not going to happen. She hadn't brought a swimsuit with her, anyway.

She smiled and nodded.

'Sounds good.'

'I expect you're tired, and you'll probably find that jet lag might kick in tomorrow, so I've made sure that nothing kicks off until late morning. You can lie in.'

'I'll be fine.'

'Have you ever done a trip of this length before to a country with this time difference?'

Helen reddened. She thought of her dad, his fussing and his worrying when she'd been younger. And then in the blink of an eye she'd been making all her girlish plans for a wedding that had never happened. In between all of that, she and George hadn't given a moment's thought to travelling anywhere, because they had been too busy putting money aside to leave their rented accommodation and buy somewhere of their own once they were married.

So much planning, and yet he had walked away, and the woman with whom he had settled down in record time had been the very opposite of Helen.

'No,' she admitted shortly.

'Then don't underestimate the effects of jet lag,' Gabriel murmured softly. He looked at her for a few long, silent seconds. 'I don't want you to feel that you have to snap to attention if you're exhausted, Helen.'

'I wouldn't do that.'

'Sure? Because everybody needs to unwind now and again, especially when they work in a high-stress environment as you do, and you won't be judged if that happens.'

With Helen making no response to that, Gabriel straightened and continued briskly, 'Right. I'll leave you to it. You can order in whatever you want and I'll let you have breakfast whenever you please tomorrow morning. You can have it delivered to the cottage, or you can head to the restaurant, which is through the clearing and straight ahead in the building alongside where we checked you in.'

'Thank you. And where and when shall we meet to head into town?'

'Eleven. Reception. My driver will be on standby to take us for our first round of meetings.'

He half-saluted with his bandaged hand, and she breathed a sigh of relief as he vanished into the night, leaving her to get on with the business of getting her thoughts in order.

Racing pulses and a foolishly hammering heart, because she happened to have been swept away from her usual safe environment for ten minutes, just weren't going to do.

She'd grown up since George and had had time to evaluate her choices and firmly establish herself as a woman with her head very firmly screwed on. Her sexy, charming boss wasn't going to mess with any of that.

Gabriel was waiting for her at eleven sharp the following morning. Helen spotted him chatting to Pammy, of the long, blonde hair, and from her heightened colour and bright eyes she could see that the twenty-something woman was thrilled to bits to have this striking Italian guy flirting with her.

Because flirting was surely what he was doing, half-leaning on the counter, with his bandaged hand making him even sexier than he already was for reasons she couldn't fathom.

Honestly. No sooner had one girlfriend disappeared through that revolving door than another potential was in the offing. Didn't the man need any breathing space at all? Ridiculous. Superficial. Typical!

She cleared her throat and looked at him coolly as he slowly turned to her, gave her the once over and then strolled unhurriedly in her direction.

Again, he was casually dressed. He wore a different pair of trousers, grey this time, and a grey-and-white-striped polo shirt with a distinctive logo on the pocket. Helen instantly felt uncomfortable and over-dressed in her dark-blue knee-length skirt and, to accommodate the heat, a short-sleeved shirt buttoned to the neck, the little pearl buttons somehow feeling like the height of frumpiness.

She had her laptop bag slung over her shoulder, along with her handbag.

'Ready?' Gabriel raised his eyebrows but said not a word about her choice of clothing, another nod to the fact that she was here to work.

'I've collated all the relevant information on the deal in one file,' she said, turning away from the flustered young girl at Reception and staring out to where the limo was waiting for them. 'I thought it would be easier than trying to retrieve strands from various places. All the documents to do with the legal side of things are in one place and I've emailed it all to you.'

'Excellent. Very efficient.'

'Have you checked?'

'Not yet, no. I'm assuming this will all go smoothly because so much fact-checking has already been done. These are mere formalities, even if there promises to be quite a bit of them. And naturally, unless they're all in order, there's still an outside chance that things might hit a roadblock. Unlikely with me at the helm,' he murmured in a low drawl. 'Bandaged hand or no bandaged hand. How did you sleep?'

'Very well. Thank you.' Helen slipped into the back seat through the door the driver had swept round to open for her. It was another glorious day and the rich, heady scent of flowers filled her nostrils. For a fleeting moment, she almost lost herself in the illusion that she wasn't here on business. The illusion didn't last long. In fact, it was comprehensively dispelled when Gabriel joined her in the back, angling his big body against the door so that he could look at her.

'This is a beautiful part of the world,' he said, snapping shut the partition and then devoting all his focused concentration on her.

Suddenly the intimate, confined space felt stifling and Helen breathed in deeply. Gabriel was very good when it came to making a person feel as though no one else in the world existed. She had seen him in action with a couple of women in the past: had seen the way he had perched on his desk when one of them had happened to drop by unannounced; had seen the way his dark eyes had lasered them to the spot until they were blushing and coyly responsive. When he'd politely but firmly ushered them out after five minutes, they hadn't seemed to feel rejected.

Even in meetings, he would focus on someone and that someone would hesitate and then do exactly as he wanted.

But with her? They worked together in absolute harmony but that focused concentration was something he had only ever applied when discussing something of a work nature. Now, for some odd reason, Helen felt a tingle of sexual awareness stir inside her and she was confused and horrified in equal measure.

She drew in a hitched breath and reminded herself that the occasional surreptitious glance at a guy who was undeniably sexy was nothing to be particularly concerned about. Yet she found herself adjusting her position to quell the tingling between her thighs.

'Yes.' She rushed into speech, but her nerves were all over the place, and her usual calm had decided to desert her. 'Your…your driver told me a lot about the place, the cafés and the restaurants, and of course the scenery is beautiful. Breath-taking—the trees and the flowers. Yes, really beautiful…' Her voice fizzled out but his eyes remained on her, pensive and, she thought, a little amused.

This wasn't her at all. She didn't do girly—never had. She had always been serious and controlled, her life running on carefully regulated tracks, but right now she felt *girly*, and it was disconcerting.

'I imagine we'll work for a couple of hours, and probably break for lunch to be brought, but what remains of the afternoon will be free.'

'Yes, well, if I have to work on the minutes then I shall be more than happy to return to the hotel if you want to stay on and enjoy whatever there is to enjoy in the city.'

'That's extremely diligent, Helen.' His dark eyes were serious and his voice was mild and thoughtful. 'Of course, I would expect nothing less. However, this came as something of a surprise for you and, that being the case, I insist that you see something of the place while you're here. There's no need to bury yourself in front of your computer. Meetings will kick off tomorrow at the same time and you can do whatever needs to be done in the morning.'

'Of course, but...'

'No buts. I'll show you around.'

Gabriel looked at her with lazy concentration, his lush lashes masking what was going through his head.

He could feel her discomfort in waves. She was dressed for the office and any deviation from the script had not been predicted. Yet how hard would it be for her to take some time out with him? What was the big deal? He didn't intimidate her. He knew that for a fact, sensed it in the way she was never afraid of telling him what she thought, even if the criticisms were always wrapped up in polite packaging he could never fault. So why the hesitation?

She was a girl in her twenties, yet she behaved like someone twice that age, and here, under a syrupy sun and an alien landscape, Gabriel was suddenly intensely curious to find out what made her tick.

Broodingly, his dark eyes roved over her, appreciating her slender, pale-skinned delicacy, the Cupid's bow of her mouth, the intelligent slant of her calm brown eyes and, dropping down, the jut of small breasts pushing against her top.

Far less than a handful, he mused.

He frowned, shifted and dragged his wayward thoughts back to what they had been talking about.

'Let's go through what we need to cover,' he said more brusquely than he intended, because somewhere in his head his thoughts were still drifting in unfamiliar waters, playing around with images that were off-limits. 'We both know how much lawyers can waffle. The less of that, the better.'

He wrapped it up fast. He felt his eyes straying to her slight form positioned just to the right of him. Out of the corner of his eye, he could see her frown and the concentration on her face as she annotated details of what was happening, pulling up relevant pieces of information at the speed of light, and printing it all off on a printer which, at his request, had been installed within touching distance.

She moved quickly, confidently and gracefully. Once or twice he asked her something, and she knew exactly where he was going with his questions and responded accordingly.

Lunch was brought and eaten while work continued, and at a little after four everything was done and dusted and there was the usual round of barely concealed self-congratulatory noises on a job well done.

Gabriel switched off. He'd sat through many a conclusion to thorny, detailed work and all he wanted to do now was relax.

'Brilliant work, Helen.'

Those were his first words to her as they left the hotel, moving from air-conditioned comfort out into the sultry summer heat.

'Thank you. It all seemed very straightforward. I'm very happy to explore on my own if you have better things to do.'

'My calendar is oddly empty,' Gabriel murmured drily.

Helen wondered whether boredom was driving him into occupying himself with second best—Plain Jane secretary because sexpot girlfriend was no longer on the scene. She could do without him feeling sorry for her, or anyone else for that matter, seeing her as a second-best filler-in when there was no one else more exciting to play with. Being ditched all those years ago had made her proud, had made her learn the value of detaching and concealing what might be going on under the surface. Gabriel's staggering self-assurance, that came from money, power and good looks, made it seem even more important that she stuck to the script and maintained her cool.

'I expect you've been here before?' she asked politely, although her attention was going this way and that, taking in the perfectly arrayed line of shops, the quaint street, the patriotic flags over doorways and the bustle of very affluent tourists.

Tall palms and swaying trees lined the streets and avenues and there was a jostling, cosmopolitan feel that was vibrant and invigorating.

'I don't tend to do the sightseeing stuff,' Gabriel admitted with a shrug and Helen briefly turned to look at him.

'I'm sorry Fifi isn't here to share it with you. That must be disappointing.'

'I find that it's no big deal.' His expression was veiled as their eyes met. 'I know this part of the world because of the vineyards I inherited, but my parents never stayed too long in one place. And I grew up in England, even though I suppose you could say that my origins were split between Italy and America. I have no issue reacquainting myself with the place on my own.'

'That must have been odd for you, never being in one place.'

'Life happens.' He closed the conversation down and, in so doing, left her wanting more.

More ground shifted from under her feet, because here they were, straying beyond their boundary lines, leaving her confused and ill at ease. Her neat skirt and blouse, which had been fine when they'd been working in the boardroom, made her feel uncomfortable and out of place.

As though reading her mind, he said gently, 'Have you brought anything more casual to wear, Helen?'

'Yes. Of course.'

'Then why don't you think about wearing it tomorrow? This is a casual sort of place. Even the lawyers were in tee-shirts and cotton trousers.'

'I...'

'And what about a swimsuit? It's hot and there's that pool, and you can't leave without using it.'

'I didn't bring one of those.' She almost heaved a sigh of relief.

'Of course. Because you're here to work.'

He was laughing at her and she suddenly felt dull and unexciting—the dutiful secretary incapable of letting her hair down. The dutiful secretary, still in her twenties, incapable of letting her hair down, which made things worse.

'Because I'm not going to be here very long and I didn't see the point of banking on time off to swan around.'

'In that case, we should remedy the situation. An hour relaxing in a pool after a hard day's work is hardly what I would call *swanning around*. It's called *recharging your batteries after slaving over reports and facts and figures without a break*.'

Helen burst out laughing.

'What's so funny?'

'You make it sound as though I've been chained to a desk, starved of food and forced to work for days on end without sleep. We had a delicious lunch brought to us, and it was a shorter than usual day, in actual fact. My batteries don't need that much recharging, as it happens.'

So he thought that she was hard-working but dull, wrapped up in doing the perfect job to the point where she had to be ordered to down tools and relax... What would he think were he ever to see a different side to her—a side that was wild and reckless? The thought took hold and it was a little scary, making her think that safety might not have been all it had always been cracked up to be.

When had she ever let herself go? she wondered. When had she ever dared to turn her back on all those life lessons that had been embedded in her from such a young age?

A thousand thoughts flitted through her head, darting like quicksilver.

George had been her rock, or so she had thought at the time, and he had also been her shield. The big, bad world was out there and he had been the protector she'd thought she needed. But as it turned out she hadn't, because she'd moved to London and managed the big, bad world just fine. Hadn't she?

Okay, so she didn't do clubs and bars. She didn't sleep around or try guys out for size. But that didn't mean that she was a bore, she thought now; didn't mean that there wasn't a sense of daring lurking beneath the surface.

For some reason, Gabriel's amused teasing, those sexy, dark eyes appraising her in these new surroundings, stirred something inside her that wanted to show him that there were sides to her that might be unexpected—wanted to show *herself* that there were sides to her that might be unexpected.

She drew in a sharp, unsteady breath.

'But you're right,' she murmured. 'I love swimming and I was always very good at it. It would be brilliant to have a dip in the pool. I haven't even seen what it's like.' She looked around her. 'There must be a shop here somewhere that sells swimsuits.'

She glanced at him and felt a stab of triumph at the momentary flash of surprise on his face. Had he thought her so predictable that she would retreat from the horror of relaxing when she was here to work? Would allow him to gently tease her, safe in the knowledge that she would always scuttle away from facing him down when it came to anything of a personal nature?

'Lots.'

'I'll have a wander around and find one.'

'I'll come with you. Like I said, I'm familiar with the area.'

'No need, Gabriel. I'm not completely at sea when it comes to exploring somewhere new.'

He stood back, fidgeted hesitantly for a few seconds and raked his fingers through his dark hair.

'I can find a shop, buy a swimsuit and make my way back all under my own steam.'

'Of course...'

'So I'll see you in the morning? I don't seem to have any jet lag at all.'

'You're very welcome to join me for dinner with Terry and his wife.'

'No thank you, Gabriel. You've said that they're long-standing friends of your parents whom you haven't seen for years and I'm sure they'll want to have you all to themselves.'

For a few seconds, their eyes tangled and she felt her breath hitch. He had amazing eyes—so dark, so piercing and so disturbing when they were pinned to her, as they were now. 'Your hand may not be in great working order but I don't think I need to come with you to cut up your food and feed you, do I?'

'Since when do you do sarcasm?'

'I'm sorry. Seldom.' Helen lowered her eyes. She wasn't sorry. She never, ever shared any personal opinions with him but something about being here, away from their usual surroundings, made her feel restless with the trajectory of her life, dissatisfied with her own predictability.

'No need to apologise,' Gabriel drawled softly, his voice sending shivers up and down her, reminding her that sometimes it felt safe to get close to the fire until you suddenly went up in flames. This? This felt a bit like getting close to a fire.

That said…she knew that she was far too controlled ever to get burnt. Buying a swimsuit, taking a dip in a pool, relaxing when she knew that her boss wasn't going to be around anyway—why should any of that constitute grounds for panic?

She'd spent over three years working with this guy, and sure she could stand back and appreciate his crazy sexiness and his charismatic allure, but she wasn't one of those blondes who swooned at his feet. She'd proven that. She was detached when it came to her boss. She would never in a million years go for someone like him which made her immune to everything about him that seemed to suck women in.

And, if he'd suddenly fired up something inside her that wanted *change*, then that wasn't a bad thing. Was it? Being careful was very different from never taking chances. What was life without taking the occasional risk? She gone down the uber-safe route with George but hadn't that been a mistake? Climbing out of her work gear and lightening up with the man now watching her through narrowed eyes was hardly going to break the bank when it came to risk taking!

'So, tomorrow...' she threw into the lengthening silence between them. 'Timings?'

'No need to rush out of bed. It will be the same routine as today.'

'Lovely.' She stepped back and made a point of looking around her. 'I'll head off now, if that's all right?'

'No reason it shouldn't be. But getting back to the hotel? Forget about taking a taxi. I'll get my driver to collect you.'

Helen smiled, shrugged, dutifully put all the details of his driver into her phone and listened politely while he gave her various helpful hints about where she could go if she fancied something to eat or drink. She frowned and stifled a sigh when, eventually, he asked her whether she was absolutely sure she was going to be okay, left to her own devices.

'I'll manage,' she said with a stiff smile, 'And, if I find I can't, I'll make sure I get on the phone and call you immediately so that you can come and rescue me.' She smiled sweetly and, wow, did it make her feel good when he shot her a disconcerted frown in response.

If there was one thing guaranteed to make her change gear, it was Gabriel de Luca treating her as someone who might be sharp as a tack in front of a computer but as clueless as the village idiot when it came to everything else...

CHAPTER THREE

IT WAS A long evening. Or rather, it felt like it. Gabriel had been distracted at the restaurant bar and then had caught himself glancing at his watch as he made small talk with Terry and Caro over lobster and champagne.

He would rearrange, make it up to them, wine and dine them another night. But he had to go…a thorny problem with a big deal…time was money…

And he *would* make it up to them—in style. After all, he hadn't seen them in a while, and he was extremely fond of them. In the preposterously lavish but uncertain world he had inhabited as a kid, they had been more of a constant than his own parents had been.

They had been neighbours, two vast estates sitting alongside one another. His parents had chosen to use their sprawling house as a base, leaving the upkeep of it to other people so that they could travel the world and do very little, aside from have fun. But Terry and Caro, considerably older, had seldom travelled, preferring to enjoy their surroundings and taking pride in everything they did to their house and its huge grounds.

The couples had met over drinks at the local members-only club and somehow it had been established, in not so many words, that Terry and his wife would somehow 'keep an eye' on Gabriel when he was on his own, with only two nannies and various employees there to supervise him.

In hindsight, Gabriel wondered what Terry and his wife had made of the situation. What had they thought of his parents who had had the freedom to indulge in one another and pursue their heady, selfish lives of uninterrupted enjoyment, in receipt of their huge passive income from family holdings which had been set up to virtually to run itself, thanks to people who had been put in place years before? They'd never said and he'd never asked. He'd formed his own conclusions about his parents all by himself.

From the age of six, he could remember the older couple swinging by for him, gathering him up to take him out for ice-cream, a meal somewhere, some fun fair or other that had been passing through or to hit some balls on the three-hole golf course they had had landscaped, because Terry had been fanatical about the game.

Through all this, his own parents had been globetrotting, descending now and again with armfuls of gifts from whatever exciting countries they'd visited. They would stay for a couple of weeks, just time to catch their breath, then once again would come the round of nannies and caretakers and, through it all, Terry and Caro picking up the slack.

At the age of eleven, he'd been shipped to boarding school in England, never to return to America to live, but always keeping up with the childless couple who had been there for him, especially following his parents' deaths. He had leant on them as a source of support in his own solitary, independent way.

So looking at his watch, being distracted enough to

wind up the evening prematurely? Unacceptable. And yet he had been on edge, his thoughts returning to his secretary and that sudden unexpected glimpse of fire simmering beneath the cool, placid surface.

One flame—the glimmer of a burning spark… How much more to see? Where had she been hiding that fire?

Somewhere deep inside, he recognised that that flame had always been there, flickering steadily behind the contained demeanour. She would lower her eyes and half-smile at something he'd said and he'd feel that feathery frisson, as though something had passed very softly over his skin.

It was a reaction no other woman had ever been able to rouse in him, and he had always uncomfortably pushed it aside, but out here… Out here, the barriers had been broken through. Heck, that was why he'd spent the evening with her in his head.

He didn't want to be curious but he was. He didn't want to think about her as a woman he wanted to touch, but he did. Had he always wanted to touch her? It was an unsettling thought. He wondered whether the fiasco with Fifi had shifted something inside him, made him confront a life spent without any commitment whatsoever. A life spent indulging his own physical desires whilst shrugging off the responsibility of taking those desires and trying to turn them into something more significant.

That was an unsettling thought. Was he so different from his parents? Wasn't all self-indulgence the same, even if no kids were involved?

He would never make the mistake of handing over his heart to anyone, of losing control emotionally, but was there some other way that didn't involve a parade of beauties coming and going without ever leaving a dent in his life?

And, underneath all those discomforting questions, the image of his quiet but curiously compelling secretary shimmered and beckoned.

He'd made his excuses and left with the sun still shining and the evening barely beginning.

He reckoned the only way to take his mind away from those forbidden places was to work. He would head back to his cottage and throw himself into work, and by morning whatever passing fever that seemed to afflict him would be gone.

Truth was, whatever passing fever this was, it *had* to go because he had no intention of doing anything that could possibly jeopardise the vital working relationship he had with his secretary. Temptation could be fought and conquered. There was no choice here.

She was the best he'd ever had. They were tuned into one another in ways that never failed to astonish him. She was so much cleverer than she probably gave herself credit for and he was amazed she hadn't taken her qualifications much further and gone to bigger, more rewarding places. Not that he was complaining. He wasn't. He made sure to pay her what she deserved and then double, ensuring loyalty.

She liked her privacy and he'd made sure never to overstep boundary lines, even though they puzzled him. Surely lightening up a little wasn't a crime? Even when she was with some of her colleagues, he could see that underneath the laughter and the gossip there was always something holding her back. Why?

That was a curiosity he had always made sure never to indulge. She was smart enough to get a damn good job anywhere and he was smart enough to make sure he kept her close. But what made her tick? Had there been a man in her life? Was there someone? No one? Surely there were guys out there who could see just what he saw—a woman with depth and substance who was as sexy as hell underneath whatever drab outfits she chose to wear?

Because they were out here didn't mean he was going to play fast and loose with three years' worth of sensible good intentions, however. And Gabriel knew himself well. *Sensible* good intentions and *women* didn't always go hand in hand. He enjoyed women. He liked the thrill of the chase and, if boredom inevitably followed, that didn't negate the thrill of the chase.

He enjoyed women but the chase always ended and that was how he liked it. Until now. Who wanted to play catch for ever? But that didn't mean the only alternative was love.

Love, to Gabriel, was a destructive force. That was what he had learnt from his own parents. It burnt like a raging fire, out of control and all-consuming. His parents had loved one another to the exclusion of everything and everyone, including him.

Why else would they have left him to his own devices from the time he'd been able to walk? They had been so involved with one another that there had been nothing left over to give him or anyone. They had both been only children, heirs to vast personal fortunes, and they had done nothing with their lives but take advantage of the privileges of their birth. Maybe, if they had needed to work, reality might have made an appearance at some point but they hadn't. They'd been the original trust-fund children with the world at their disposal.

And love? It had made them selfish and single-minded.

It was a blessing they had both died together because he was sure that neither would have survived for long without the other. If the only people they'd needed were each other, then removing one would have killed the other. So, love? *Thanks, but no thanks.* The thought of ever putting himself in the position of being vulnerable in a life where his heart made the decisions and his head obeyed was repugnant.

Yes, there had been other examples of love. Terry and Caro were one of them, but they were few and far between, and for Gabriel the very prospect of handing himself over to someone else was to be avoided at all costs.

He could identify with Helen's need for control because it was a trait he shared with her.

Maybe, down the line, he would contemplate marriage, which admittedly had certain advantages—who could maintain a revolving carousel of women for ever? But, as and when that time came, it would be a well-considered situation with a woman with whom the primary aim would be compatibility—two adults who got along. No highs and lows, no agonising and no vulnerability. Affection made a lot more sense than love, and even he knew that the time came when passion ran its course.

So the women in his life came and went and he never bothered to fight temptation when it came to sex. Two consenting adults made for a very happy equation. He never made promises he couldn't keep and never spoke about a future he knew wouldn't happen. Only now had the ground begun to shift under his feet.

It was frustrating to realise that he was somehow starting to think of Helen as more than just the quiet, understated woman who worked so well alongside him; beginning to see what he had successfully managed to ignore for three years. But he couldn't afford to think of her in any other terms. He would have to make sure his head did the thinking and his body did the obeying.

The hotel was quiet when he arrived back, his chauffeur-driven car noiselessly circling the courtyard to deliver him in front of the flamboyant flowering trees that guarded the reception and the various pathways that led to the clusters of cottages on the grounds.

It was still warm, although the sun was beginning to dip. He headed straight for his quarters, brushing past the exuberantly romantic canopy of trees, thinking ahead to what he could accomplish in the hours ahead.

He was barely looking left or right.

The romance of the setting was beginning to get on his nerves. His erstwhile girlfriend might have thought long and hard about finding the right place to seduce him into the sort of commitment he had no intention of making, and he might have found it reasonably charming, had she still been on the scene minus unreasonable demands. But, given the circumstances, all this lush foliage, mouth-watering scenery and tantalising shaded pathways were a nuisance. When his thoughts were all over the place, the last thing he needed was damn romance.

In the midst of brushing some blossoms from his shirt, he stilled at the faint sound of water, of splashing. Someone was swimming in the pool behind the cottages.

Gabriel hesitated.

But then curiosity got the better of him, and he was irritated with himself even as he followed the path that wound alongside the cottages. It nestled amidst stunted trees and over-sized flowering shrubbery in a way that had been artfully created to give the illusion of it being hewn from the rocks, stones and earth through which it threaded, rather than purposefully engineered by men in hard hats sitting in digger trucks.

He knew what he was expecting. He half-hoped that he was wrong; that the splashing, which was barely a sound quivering in the still air, came from other occupants eager to take advantage of the late-summer warmth and sunshine.

He emerged by the pool and stood completely still.

She was as graceful in the water as a fish, her slender body encased in a black one-piece, slicing through the blue-green, barely needing to tilt her head to draw breath.

Gabriel felt he had never seen anything like it.

How could dreary office suits and buttoned-up blouses conceal a body that was so slender and so perfectly proportioned? Even as she moved, he could make out strong, well-shaped legs, arms that carried definition and the curve of her narrow waist.

He breathed in sharply, unable to move forward but incapable of beating a retreat. Images that had been playing in his head coalesced into a reality that was a thousand times more alluring. Standing in the shade of overhanging trees, he watched and then flushed when she came to a stop by the side of the pool, her hand on the *faux* mossy ledge, and turned towards the cottages.

He should have walked away when he'd had the chance. *Too late.*

Their eyes tangled and eventually he propelled himself forward, because heading towards her in a natural and easy manner seemed the better of two options, the other being shiftily skulking off in plain sight.

'I see you decided to try the pool,' he drawled, when he was within earshot.

The pool, shaped to resemble a very large pond, was

dappled from the setting sun slanting through the over-hanging trees.

Her hair was wet and clung to her cheeks and her skin was smooth and flawless.

'What are you doing here? I thought you were having dinner with your friends.'

'Work.' He pulled across one of the wooden chairs, largely the only concession to the fact that this was actually a swimming pool and not a natural body of water in the middle of a glade. He sat and promptly leaned forward, his arms resting on his thighs. 'Thought I'd cut short the evening and see if I could work through some of the details that still need ironing out. How's the water?'

'Please don't let me keep you if you've returned to work.'

'Maybe I'll join you. I haven't been in since I got here, and it's a nice evening for it.'

Damn, he couldn't take his eyes off her. How had he not paid more attention to just how huge her eyes were? How long, lush and dark her eyelashes? Or how her mouth was so beautifully full and defined?

'I was just getting out, as it happens.'

Helen could have kicked herself. What had possessed her to say that?

One minute she'd been swimming, loving the glide of cool water over her and the peaceful, noiseless silence of the pool. But the next, there he was, lounging against one of the trees, his hand indolently shoved in the pocket of his loose cream trousers, looking every inch the sophisticated billionaire.

Shock at seeing him had ripped through her, bringing her out in goose bumps. He'd walked towards the side of the pool and, the closer he'd come, the more her nervous system had plunged into disarray.

She felt exposed. Here in the deep end, she was treading water, one hand on the ledge to support herself. The pool might have been fashioned to replicate a pond, but the water was chlorinated and clear as crystal, and she was horribly aware of the distorted image of her swimsuit-clad body under the surface.

'Were you?'

'I…'

'I'm very sorry if I interrupted your enjoyment. Feel free to ignore me. I'll sit here and take the weight off before I head in to work. What did you do about dinner?'

'Gabriel, I haven't eaten yet and—and I'm just about to head in.'

'You haven't *eaten* yet?'

'Gabriel…'

'I blame myself!'

'What are you talking about?' Treading water whilst trying to ignore the movement of her body under the surface was exhausting but the man showed no sign of going anywhere.

'You're far too polite, Helen. There's no need to feel awkward about ordering room service or going to the restaurant to eat!'

'Whoever said anything about feeling awkward?'

'Of course, I'm just glad that you decided to drop the work routine for five minutes so that you could enjoy this pool—and, I must say, you seem to be a very strong swimmer. But I hope you weren't thinking of grabbing something from the mini-bar in the cottage and working after hours!'

Helen was beginning to feel a little cold now that she

was no longer burning energy swimming. The light was fading fast and shadows were beginning to replace the dappling of the setting sun.

She began levering herself out, self-conscious and clumsy, feeling his dark eyes boring into her, and she was rudely brought to her senses when he reached out with his un-bandaged hand and effortlessly hoisted her to her feet. He simultaneously stood up and she stumbled into him as she lost her balance, trying to sweep her hair from her eyes and extract her captured hand at one and the same time.

She reached out, flattened her palm against his chest and almost passed out. His tough, masculine body was as hard as steel, his chest tightly packed with well-honed muscle and, in his nearness, came the fragrant aroma of whatever woody aftershave he used.

For a fleeting second, she breathed him in, nostrils flaring, swept up in a moment of searing heat and a hot, sexual awareness that shocked and terrified her.

She raised alarmed eyes to his and was ensnared by the glittering, dark depths of his, and the way they drifted from hers to her mouth and lingered there. He reached and traced the contour of her mouth in a shockingly intimate gesture.

It lasted a second then he dropped his hand as she sprang back, almost stumbling again. But, instead of releasing her, he held her arm, although at least their bodies were further apart and her addled brain had a chance to clear.

'You okay?'

'Of course I am!'

'Good, because we don't need another invalid.' He held up his bandaged hand and waved it but his eyes were focused on her, deep, dark and riveting. And not obeying any of the parameters they had in place, trampling all over the work boundaries that were never, ever crossed.

Or was she just imagining that? Because, right now, her fevered senses could be getting up to who only knew what tricks of the imagination. She hadn't imagined the touch of his finger on her mouth, though. That was seared into her mind with the red-hot burn of a branding iron.

She was breathing fast, as if she'd been running a marathon.

'Let me go!' She yanked her hand away and he stepped back.

Gabriel had never felt tension like this in his life. The charge flowing between them was electric. She'd been in his head, sending his thoughts in a tailspin, and now here she was and every pore in his body yearned to touch.

'My apologies,' he said huskily. His voice was cool and controlled but his thoughts were all over the place, and he could feel the steady pain of his erection shamelessly pushing against the zip of his trousers.

Helen spun round and ducked to fetch her towel. The swimsuit was clammy against her body and she was aware of the tautness of her nipples against the damp fabric, stiff, sensitive and achingly responsive.

She took a few steady breaths and reminded herself that this was her boss. *Her boss!*

She would do well to remember *that* little technicality!

'I'll head in now.'

'Of course.' Gabriel turned and began heading away from the pool. He could *feel* her tripping alongside him, but he didn't dare look at her, because one more glance and that erection, which was thankfully beginning to subside, would barrel into life again. Had she noticed the bulge under the trousers? If so, she gave no sign.

He clenched his jaw. In his mind he saw the fall of her small breasts as she had leant to retrieve her towel from where she had hung it on the low branch of a tree by the side of the pool. What the hell had possessed him to touch her like that? It had lasted a second, but still—there was no excuse. Since when had he ever allowed his body to control his head?

He delivered her to her door and watched as she fumbled to fetch the key from the cloth bag she had taken to the pool.

An urgency to straighten that kink in their otherwise smooth relationship was suddenly overpowering and, before she stepped through the door and shut it on him, he placed his flattened palm on it and followed her through.

'What are you doing?'

Helen swivelled to face him and took a couple of steps back. She'd wrapped the towel around her waist but was conscious of her upper half and the scant cover provided by the swimsuit. She didn't want to think about it, but she was well aware that her cleavage was on display, such as it was, the shadow dipping into the V of the swimsuit.

She folded her arms and stared at him, heart thumping and mouth going dry. He'd never looked at her like this. His dark eyes were narrowed with intent. She longed for the safety of her work clothes, her laptop in its neat little case, an office chair in front of a desk—a great, big desk which would provide much-needed distance between them, a much-needed physical barrier, reminding them of their roles.

Reminding *her* of *her* role—because right now she was suffocating from the weight of his presence. Even when she'd been engaged to George—had thought he was the one for her—he had never made her feel like this. He had never made her feel as though she was going to burst out of her own skin, as though every square inch of her body had suddenly been sensitised.

She hated Gabriel for making her feel things she didn't want to feel. Was it just this damned place with its heavy scents, leafy glades and fairy lights all over the place? Was this what had stirred a recklessness inside her, or had that recklessness been waiting in the shadows for just the right time to appear? And, if it had, why on earth did it have to manifest itself with this particular man?

But she knew why. There'd been those little sidelong glances over the years...the hum of electricity when he'd got too close... She'd hidden behind her prim work clothes, kept her guard up, but nothing had been able to stop her eyes from wandering and her mind from playing games.

'Please leave,' she said tightly.

Gabriel raked his fingers through his hair.

'Back there, at the pool...'

'I don't want to talk about this.'

'I—I touched you and that was inexcusable. I have no idea what came over me.'

'I don't know what you're talking about. I'm beginning to feel cold and I think it's time you went back to your—your room. Didn't you say you returned early so that you could do some work?'

'Helen...'

'No!'

They stared at one another and the silence was so thick, she could almost hear the wild beating of her heart.

'Nothing happened there. *Nothing.*'

'If that's how you want to play it,' Gabriel muttered, 'Then it's not a problem. Nothing did happen there but, just in case you were to revisit that conclusion, I want to assure you that...' he breathed in deeply '...that nothing will ever happen. That... I don't know what that was, but I value you too much to ever jeopardise your position as my employee.'

Helen knew that she should breath a sigh of relief that normal play had been resumed but she was still in another place and his reassurances, instead of relaxing her, made her feel angry and defiant.

He'd made an easy assumption that he could apologise his way out of that touch, the fleeting touch that had sent her into a panicked tailspin—that he could shrug and smile a crooked, bemused smile and muse that why he'd succumbed to that brief, out-of-character gesture was a mystery. *What the heck had that been about?* he would have asked himself with genuine puzzlement.

Of course he'd have no idea what that had all been about! He'd let his eyes wander over her swimsuit-clad body—and she didn't get why, because she certainly wasn't the sort of woman he would usually be attracted to. He'd had a momentary lapse in concentration because she'd taken him by surprise—because she wasn't in one of her usual working outfits, which always seemed to amuse him. And, naturally, he hadn't hesitated because he was a guy who was utterly assured in his ability to attract. It probably wouldn't have occurred to him that he might get knocked back.

Instinct trumped common sense. The urge to step out of the box, for once, was overwhelming.

'Thank you for that,' she said stiffly, biting down that temptation because, at the end of the day, she worked for him and discretion was certainly going to be the better part of valour.

But it was a struggle.

'I mean it, Helen. I respect you. I respect your boundaries. Like I said, I had no idea...' He shuffled and looked away, frowning, for a couple of seconds. 'I don't know what to say.'

'Nothing,' Helen muttered in a driven undertone, her small hands clenched into angry fists. 'Don't say anything.'

He ignored her. 'Let's just say we put this behind us and move on. I just wanted to set the record straight because I don't want you to feel uncomfortable, either here or when we return to London. You have my word.'

Helen gritted her teeth. She didn't know how they had managed to arrive at this quagmire but she felt as though, having got here, she either waded through it and emerged on the other side by standing up to him or she allowed herself to sink without defending herself. The latter option made sense but the former was irresistible.

'You have an ego the size of a planet, do you know that?'

'Come again?'

'You took me by surprise,' she conceded hotly, colour flaring into her cheeks. 'But you don't have to make a big deal of it. You don't have to bend over backwards to reassure me that it won't be repeated. I'm not going to shrivel up in trepidation whenever I'm with you. You're not my type, Gabriel. I work for you. You're my boss and the reason we work well together is that I'm not like—like—all those women who can't get enough of you.'

'I merely wanted to reassure you—'

'I'm not attracted to you!'

'No, I never said you were,' he muttered. 'Did I?'

For a couple of treacherous seconds, Helen was almost tempted to smile. Firstly, she'd never seen her boss so discomfited before, and secondly, the very thought of someone not finding him attractive was obviously a concept he hadn't quite taken on board. His mouth was saying one thing, his awkward scowl and dark flush were saying another.

'Want the truth?' she continued, side-stepping the diplomacy she had been determined to hang onto. 'I don't approve of your behaviour with women.'

'Sorry?'

'I know I probably shouldn't be saying this but, now that we're clearing the air, I feel I should make my position completely clear so that you don't have any misunderstandings.'

'I'm all ears.'

'I don't have a lot of time for guys who play the field.' She crossed her arms and watched as his mouth fell open and he stared at her with narrow-eyed incredulity. His quiet, obedient secretary had opinions! She felt a surge of satisfaction, which was far more powerful than any fear she felt at saying things she might live to regret. 'You think I'm helpless. Or maybe hopeless would be a better description.'

'That's ridiculous!'

'Is it? You think I'm so gullible that one passing touch from you and I risk falling apart at the seams from now on. You think I'm utterly wet behind the ears when it comes to the opposite sex!'

'Are you?'

'No, I'm not! I was once engaged, if you really want to know!'

Gabriel's mouth fell open and he stared. Helen bitterly regretted every word that had passed her lips. All her caution had gone down the drain in a single explosive confession.

'What happened? You never breathed a word...'

'Because it's none of your business, Gabriel! The fact is, I can handle what happened just then! You needn't fear that I'm going to go to pieces!'

'What happened? Didn't it work out?'

'Again, none of your business! I told you that because— because I wanted to reassure you that I just don't go for guys like you. So, there—we can now just consider this matter over and done with.'

'If you say so.' Gabriel shot her a slanting look.

'I do! So, if you'll excuse me...?'

'Of course.'

He began heading for the door. Every rebellious word she had uttered had whetted his appetite to hear more. An engagement? The depths he had glimpsed were now even more dangerously compelling.

He wasn't her type. Then who was? The guy she'd been engaged to? Was she still broken-hearted? Who the hell had the guy been? She'd probably been out of his league. It took a strong guy to deal with a strong woman and not be intimidated.

He'd done the decent thing and rushed in to reassure her that there was no need for her to be nervous around him. He'd laid it on thick about respecting her, and he'd been one hundred per cent honest. What had he expected her response to be? She might be reserved by nature, but she had opinions, and he knew that. When he replayed his little speech in his head, he could hear how patronising he might have sounded, even though that hadn't been his intention.

That said, he hadn't expected her to voice her opinions with such heat. He wanted to quiz her on what she'd said, prolong the conversation, find out more about her past.

Dangerous territory.

She'd laid it down—nothing had happened. He would go along with that because allowing curiosity to get the better of him was not something he could afford to do. He shakily accepted that conclusion.

'Tomorrow...' He turned to her, one hand on the door, halfway out.

'I'll have everything ready and on hand to print for signatures. I'll make sure those niggling discrepancies are highlighted and ironed out. When Mr Diaz is ready to sign off, everything will be in place. Will we meet at the same time—eleven?'

She tilted her head to one side. Her eyes were cool and remote. The professional hat was back in place and Gabriel could scarcely reconcile his crisply spoken secretary with the woman who had stilled for a second as he'd touched her mouth; or with the woman who had let her fires rage at him for temporarily putting her nose out of joint. The woman who had been hiding a past from him he would never have expected.

Was he really not her type?

That physical response—surely it hadn't been one-sided? Yes, he'd touched her, but she'd responded—and it hadn't just been a case of being taken by surprise, as she'd claimed.

Did her aggressive denial of any attraction conceal a forbidden urge to touch him? Was that something she'd carefully hidden over the months and years, something she refused to acknowledge? Or was this his ego talking?

Did the lady protest too much?

It was one thing to have a clear idea of what the perfect guy might look like, and maybe she'd had that perfect guy before it had all fallen apart for whatever reason. But he was no more, and who knew? Maybe she was drawn against her will to the imperfect one…

Pointless speculation, of course.

'Eleven it is.' He mock-saluted her and looked at her from under sooty lashes. 'It's all coming along very nicely. I don't foresee anything cropping up to throw this off course so, with a good following wind, you'll be back in Blighty the day after tomorrow and you can put all of this behind you…'

CHAPTER FOUR

'RIGHT.' GABRIEL SLAMMED shut his laptop and pushed himself back from the conference table at which were seated the five crucial players responsible for fine-tuning all the nuts and bolts on the deal he had just concluded. There were two highly qualified accountants, one specialising in tax, and two company lawyers to make sure every detail was in place.

And his secretary, sitting to the right of him, diligently taking minutes and printing out every piece of paper still awaiting Diaz's signature. Every so often, in her low, modulated voice, she pointed out things that might be questionable because, as she explained, Arturio wasn't au fait with modern-day tech-speak and altering the language slightly might work better for him.

This was how they worked—in tandem. Everything, was back in place, Gabriel thought, and all was right in the world.

Except…

He couldn't get rid of that memory of her from two days ago when he'd surprised her swimming in the pool… and then after, the blazing fire in her eyes when she'd told him what she thought of his lifestyle choices. And the proud tilt of her head when she'd informed him in a cool, husky voice that he wasn't her type, that she could look after herself, that she'd been engaged. She hadn't just broken through the neat little barriers she'd built up between them, the ones he'd taken care to keep in place for fear of losing her, she'd comprehensively obliterated them, wiped her hands in satisfaction and then promptly announced that the matter had been settled, to be put behind them and forgotten for ever.

He'd made sure not to utter a word about what had happened. He had seen her the day after and they had resumed their working relationship as though that blip had never taken place.

She was polite, friendly and, of course, as efficient as always... But, when he slid his eyes to the side, he could see her smooth fingers resting on the keyboard of her laptop, as though she might be on the verge of typing something, and he had to stop his imagination from going into overdrive. If he shifted just a few inches, he would be able to brush against her arm. He was desperate to know more about her and equally desperate to steer clear of asking.

'I'm seeing Arturio tomorrow,' he began, standing up and, on cue, everyone followed suit, packing away stuff and hurriedly shuffling to their feet. 'And everything is now ready for his paw print on the dotted line. I don't foresee any hitches, and that's down to a joint effort here. I want to thank you all for your hard work...'

He looked around him. They were a couple of guys in their fifties, serious and highly experienced in complex buy-outs, and the other two in their early thirties, fresh-faced and keen. He'd noticed the way those two had both slyly glanced at Helen every so often. One of them was married, with a ring on his finger. Hadn't stopped his eyes from wandering Gabriel had gritted his teeth and said nothing. Of course.

'It's...' he glanced at his watch '...not yet five. I suggest we celebrate with some champagne and an early dinner.'

There were murmurs of consent as Gabriel knew there would be. When he issued invitations, whatever the nature of the invitation, acceptance was generally a given.

'If you don't mind...'

Helen's polite voice right next to him brought him to an abrupt standstill.

'I'll give it a miss. I fly out tomorrow and I still have packing to get through. I'm sorry I'll miss seeing Arturio.'

He turned and frowned, and she smiled serenely back at him as she continued busying herself, stuffing her laptop into the bag and faffing with the lightweight coat she'd neatly draped over the back of her chair. Her working wardrobe was firmly in place. Forget about the casual look he'd recommended—she wore a knee-length blue skirt, blue-and-white-striped shirt tucked into the waistband of the skirt and flat canvas shoes.

What had her fiancé been like—safe, steady? Wouldn't she see a guy like that as the opposite of him? Safe, steady...dared he say, a little on the dull side?

'You're part of this team,' he said grittily, in a low undertone.

'I'll make sure everything's ready by tomorrow, so all Arturio has to do is sign on the dotted line.'

'Helen...'

'My flight's in the evening, so there'll be time if I have to implement any changes.'

'If you're sure,' Gabriel said gruffly, knowing very well that she'd cleverly put him on the spot. He shuffled, raked his fingers through his hair and decided that it made no difference whether his secretary came or not.

Better if she didn't!

She was suddenly a distraction on a blockbuster scale and, the faster he got over that, the better. He might just tack on an extra week out here, catch up with Terry and his wife and check out the vineyards again. He could spend more time with Arturio when he saw him—quality time, nothing about vineyards or work.

He had asked about his family, which had been like asking about strangers, in a way, yet oddly satisfying. He'd had some pieces of a past he'd never known slotted into place. He'd rather like more of those pieces slotted in. He was beginning to find out what it meant to have a family, even if it was late in the day. It meant more to him than he could have imagined. So, yes, he and Arturio—it would be good.

It would also give his body time to recover from its unexpected response to a woman who was off-limits. He would make it back to London with his head screwed back on.

'I'm sure.'

'Come on, Helen…' A coaxing plea came from one of the young lawyers and Gabriel's teeth snapped together at the smile she flashed the guy—half-distracted, half-amused, full-wattage.

'Looks like you have an admirer,' he said tightly, dropping his voice.

'Nice, isn't it?' She was already making her way to the door, saying the usual goodbyes, shaking hands and laughing at something or other one of the older guys said, something about 'should she ever need a job this side of the pond'.

How had he not noticed just how dynamic she was in her own, very special, low-key way?

'He's a lawyer,' Gabriel returned, standing back with her while the rest filed out of the conference room, talking amongst themselves. 'I'd take what the guy says with a pinch of salt.'

'Thank you for your concern.' Her face fell into a wry smile. 'You're actually not telling me anything I didn't already know.'

Gabriel smiled back at her and there was a moment of perfectly shared compatibility.

Helen's breath caught in her throat. If she took away the surge of sexual attraction that had sprung up between them, and took away all these weird, disturbing interactions that had muddied the calm water between them, and what she got was this—the sort of easy familiarity where words were unnecessary and where entire conversations could be had in just one exchanged glance.

'You must be looking forward to having some time with Arturio, Gabriel.'

He'd told her of the family connection and now he flushed, before admitting seriously, 'I am, as it happens. Might make some time after everything's done and dusted to spend a little time with him.'

'You should.'

'Thank you for sharing your opinion with me.' But he was half-smiling. 'And, now we're in sharing mode, tell me what happened between you and your fiancé.'

'Gabriel...'

'What was his name?'

'People are waiting for you.'

'Not that I can see. Well?'

'George. His name was George.'

'What happened? And I can see that you want to tell me that it's none of my business.'

'Well, it isn't, as it happens.' But she was tempted. Barriers eroded, doors opened—what harm could it do? It was hardly a state secret. 'It didn't work out. We were very young and, before we could tie the knot, he came to his senses and broke it off.' She gazed away with a little frown. 'And, if he hadn't, I would have.'

Gabriel didn't say anything. Her reticence made sense. He wanted to pursue the conversation and ask her for details, but she was right when she'd said that the rest of the crew would be waiting for him.

The rest of the crew, including the guy with his eyes on stalks. Had her thoughts begun to drift to resuming her single life, with her ex firmly behind her? Had the weird romance of the place turned her thoughts away from work and onto play? The place had certainly got to him. Had it got to her as well?

'Lost for words, Gabriel?' She had an insane desire to pull the tiger's tail. 'Maybe I needed a little break like this. It's certainly been very relaxing, having a handsome young guy flirt with me. Course, I told him I wasn't going to be here long enough to go out with him.'

She felt her skin prickle as again she ventured into foreign territory. She told herself that there was nothing outrageous about this conversation. It only felt outrageous because of the working relationship they had cultivated over the years, one in which personal things had seldom been mentioned.

'Who knows? Maybe if I'd been out here a little longer, I might have been inclined to go on that date he asked me on.'

'Go on a *date*? The guy asked you on a date?'

'It's what single people do. You should know that better than anyone else. Don't look so horrified, Gabriel.'

Gabriel relaxed and shot her a slow smile. 'It certainly is what single people do, Helen; and if I look a little startled maybe it's because I'm suddenly seeing a side to you you've been so busy keeping under wraps before. Maybe I'm liking this new side to you.'

Helen blushed and tried to recover lost ground because his soft, lazy drawl made her skin tingle and reminded her of how his finger had felt on her mouth.

'I should go.' She backed away. 'I have a lot to do.'

Gabriel raised his eyebrows. He was still grinning, a wicked grin that got to all parts of her. 'If you're quite sure you won't join us…'

'I'll see you tomorrow, Gabriel. Let me know if there are any amendments you need me to do before I submit everything.'

He watched her vanish through the revolving door into the summer sunshine, as slender and graceful as a ballerina.

Drinks and an early dinner didn't hold a huge amount of appeal, but he had to show his thanks to the hard work the guys had put in. He would go beyond and arrange a weekend for they and their families—somewhere suitably luxurious. He would doubtless use their skills again at some point and loyalty was a great thing.

He thought of one of those guys sneakily making a pass at his secretary and it made his teeth snap together. Yet she was perfectly correct—he *had* urged her to relax, to let her hair down, and if her back story had come as a shock it was only because he hadn't credited her with such a riveting one.

Broken engagements, shattered hearts... What next?

She'd never given him the slightest inclination that she was somehow trapped in a physical deep-freeze. He'd just read the outward signs and come up with his own, as it turned out incorrect, interpretation of the woman who worked so diligently and uncomplainingly for him.

And he was honest enough to admit to himself there might be just the tiniest bit of egotism behind those assumptions. He knew the power of his own personal magnetism. He'd cultivated it from a young age, flung into a boarding school on the opposite side of the world when he'd just been a kid. He'd learned that, to avoid being bullied, side-lined or mocked as an outsider with a foreign accent, it was imperative that he was accepted and, beyond acceptance, that he was admired and, ultimately, feared and respected.

He'd been clever, athletic and had learned to charm. It had been a very successful front for those feelings of hurt buried deep inside him. The hurt at how his wealthy parents had treated him had felt a lot like abandonment.

It was something he'd taken for granted over the years and he wondered, now, whether that was why he'd rushed to foregone conclusions.

Had he thought that his perfect secretary wouldn't be able to resist the occasional remark? Wouldn't be able to resist the force of his personality when he'd initially tried to tease casual chit-chat out of her? He hated to think that his ego was as big as she'd informed him she found it, in no uncertain terms, but he had to concede that there had surely been a reason he hadn't just accepted the obvious.

She was a sexy woman with a very healthy personal life who just didn't want him involved in it on any level.

Especially seeing that she'd written him off as a womaniser who played the field—probably from the very beginning, he figured.

He was half-occupied with those thoughts during the course of drinks and dinner, which was much earlier than he would usually eat, because the older guys needed to get back to their homes.

All were instantly grateful at the suggestion about a long weekend with partners and, when he magnanimously told them to agree on where they wanted to go and his secretary would sort it out, they beamed from ear to ear. 'Something beachy in Mexico' was suggested as they gathered their belonging to leave.

He called Helen the second he was on his way back.

'A couple of things to discuss...'

'Sure.'

Helen listened while he discussed two points belatedly raised over drinks, neither of which were in any way crucial to the deal, but both of which could be sorted in five minutes with an alteration to some of the wording.

She'd returned to the cottage with the sun still shining and so little packing to do that she'd finished it in under five minutes.

She should have stayed. She'd shared a bit of herself with him but then, all of a fluster, she'd made a point of leaving and afterwards had felt a bit of a fool. Now here he was, coolly talking about work, because the fluster had been all on her part...

'There's also a little trip I want you to arrange for me,'

she surfaced to hear him saying. 'A weekend somewhere. I'll fill you in on the details at a later date, but a beach somewhere expensive in Mexico looks like a likely candidate.

'This can all wait, to be honest, until tomorrow morning,' he added.

Helen had frozen at the mention of Mexico and a weekend away. That had all the hallmarks of one of his romantic rendezvous and she wondered who the latest blonde might be. Surely not...?

There was a sour taste in her mouth when she thought about it and it horrified her to think that that sour taste was plain, old-fashioned jealousy. She'd opened the door a crack and now look at the result!

'No,' she said sharply, 'It's no bother for me to sort everything out this evening. It's not even eight yet.'

'Don't you want to relax on your last night here?'

'I can come to the meeting room; just let me know what time you'd like me there.'

'Helen, there's no need for such formality. You don't have to take notes. I can just verbally brief you. I really shouldn't have interrupted your evening but I'm on my way back now. Probably have a drink on the veranda at the cottage. It was a ludicrously early dinner, but the older guys wanted to head off.'

'I'll come to your cottage. You can fill me in. It's no bother at all.'

How had it been professional to scuttle off like a scalded cat earlier? Did she want him to get the impression that he got under her skin? That he made her feel hot and bothered? She'd told him about her broken engagement because she'd wanted to point out that she wasn't an ingénue, utterly clueless about the ways of the world.

So why was she behaving like one? Why was she letting him get to her like this?

She had to play it cool. She had worked late into the night in his office many times, with a takeout between them as they had pored over whatever thorny issues required completion to a deadline. Twice, she had been summoned to his magnificent house in Holland Park, and had worked in his home office there for a couple of hours, because he'd had everything set up for complex coordination of external meetings on different time zones.

She'd never run scared on any of those occasions! Why should it bother her now to sit outside with him and go through stuff for half an hour? To be her usual unflappable, reliable self?

'Fine. Meet me there in half an hour. That suit?'

'Yes,' she said firmly. 'That suits me fine.'

Gabriel was having a whisky when he heard Helen knock and sauntered out to open the door to her.

He wasn't sure why he'd called her. Nothing needed to be done as a matter of urgency. That said, as he pulled open the door he was glad he'd made the call, because the evening suddenly seemed a little less insipid.

She'd changed into a pair of faded, light jeans and wore a tee shirt that hung loosely to the waist so that, if she raised her arms, he would be able to see a sliver of skin.

And, of course, she'd come armed with her trusty laptop. Gabriel didn't mind. He stepped aside and she swept past him straight into the small living area before spinning round to face him.

'So...'

At her brisk, no-nonsense voice, he smiled and was suddenly at ease in himself.

'Drink? I'm on the veranda at the back. Splendid view, even with the sun fading. They've done clever things with the lighting so that it's somehow possible to see for quite some distance before everything disappears into fields and open land.'

He spun round on his heels and she followed but, instead of following him out, she plonked her bag and belongings on the table in the living area and took up residence on one of the chairs, ready and poised to take notes.

A drink? A romantic view from his veranda? A twilight vista studded with fairy lights in the trees and twinkling stars in a velvet-dark sky? *No, thanks.* Table in the living area bathed in bright overhead lighting? *Yes, please.*

He got the message and sat opposite her, but the way he sprawled in the chair somehow detracted from the business-like atmosphere she was aiming for.

He talked to her about the tweaks she would have to make to the wording of the agreement, which would then be perfect and waiting only for final approval from Arturio.

It was straightforward.

Helen relaxed.

'And,' she said, tweaks done, 'You mentioned something about Mexico?' Her voice was clipped as she reached into her laptop bag for the slim notebook she always kept there.

'Ah, yes.'

Gabriel sipped his drink and eyed her over the rim of the glass, noting the faint tinge of colour pinking her cheeks.

'If you tell me the sort of thing you have in mind, I can make the necessary arrangements.'

'I've never actually been to Mexico,' he said, dumping

his squat glass on the table and then relaxing back with his hands folded behind his head. 'Don't suppose *you* have?'

'I haven't, as it happens,' Helen returned politely. 'Although I'm struggling to see what that has to do with anything.'

Gabriel decided that he very much liked this new version of his secretary—polite but a different sort of polite from what had been on offer before. A more nuanced and *impolite* polite, if there was such a thing. The politeness of someone who'd opened up and probably regretted it. The politeness of someone who had tossed him titbits of her past which had really inflamed his senses. It challenged something in him and was as invigorating as the fizz of expensive champagne after a diet of soda water.

'If you had to go there—for a long weekend—what sort of thing would you say would appeal to you?'

It was a provocative statement…and yet Gabriel didn't regret asking the question because he enjoyed the way her colour deepened, and the way she suddenly fiddled with the ring on her finger and then lowered her eyes to stare at the blank page of the notebook on her lap.

What was going through her head?

He knew what was going through her head. *He knew women. And he knew her.*

He was treading on thin ice, and he had no intention of continuing the trek to see what was on the other side.

'Beaches?' he prompted, voice oozing suggestiveness, dark eyes lazy, slumberous and amused. 'Sun setting when the violet hour comes on waves crashing on sand on an empty coastline? The distant sound of coconut trees swaying on a night breeze?'

'I had no idea you were so poetic,' Helen said shortly.

'I sometimes surprise myself,' Gabriel murmured in response.

'Well, I'm sorry, but I can't help you on this. If you want to take your new girlfriend somewhere romantic, then you'll have to come up with the destination by yourself, and of course I'll make all the necessary arrangements.'

'Oh?' Gabriel's eyebrows shot up. 'Is that what you think I'm doing—new girlfriend? How fast do you think I work? That's very cynical of you, Helen, I must say.'

'Why else would you want a romantic getaway in Mexico? Look, I don't care what you do, but please don't expect me to have input into the itinerary.'

'Would it bother you?'

'Yes, of course I would rather not do that!'

'Why?' he queried softly.

'Because…'

Helen looked at him, their eyes collided and she suddenly felt the ground collapse from under her feet. Those eyes, the amused tilt of his head, the sexuality emanating from him in waves that made her feel giddy… She found it hard to think in a straight line.

'Because?'

'Because that's not in my brief, Gabriel, and you know it isn't. So don't…don't…'

'I absolutely agree one hundred per cent, even though you've never complained before about it not being in your brief!' he retorted, standing to fetch himself another drink and then returning to the table. But he perched against it, drink in his hand, sipping and looking at her with the sort of focused intensity that would make any woman's head turn to mush.

'You do?'

'I wasn't talking about you arranging a weekend for me and a woman!' He dismissed the notion with a wave of his hand.

'Then, I don't understand.'

'The guys who were working on the deal—I told them, as a reward for some admirable focused, precision work, I would treat them to a long weekend, partners included, at a place of their choice. They came up with Mexico.'

Helen stared at him for a few seconds in open-mouthed silence.

He'd been toying with her. He'd introduced that conversation about a weekend in Mexico to…what?…gauge her reaction? He was clever when it came to the opposite sex. She'd told him that that silly business of a couple of evenings ago was nothing, nothing at all, but had he believed her? She'd let him into a sliver of her past so that he could see that she was a woman well able to deal with emotions, but had he believed her?

She snapped shut the notebook, seething with anger, and flew to her feet. She was stuffing everything into her laptop when she felt his hand on her wrist, a gentle pressure that made her skin burn.

He knew that he had an effect on her, whatever the heck she'd said, she thought in panic. It defied all common sense but she found the man attractive and now, over here, the door between them had opened a crack and he had been given an opportunity to peer through, to see that weakness inside her.

She snatched her bag from the table and stormed towards the door of the cottage.

'Helen…'

'This isn't funny.' She whipped round to look at him

and wished she hadn't because, even fuming as she was, she was still overwhelmed by his beauty, by the force of his personality, by the dark, mesmeric depths of his eyes. By a pull that was rooted in much more than superficial physical attraction, whether she faced up to that or not.

'No, it's not.'

She had moved towards the door but he was blocking her way out and, knowing that, he shifted because he didn't want her to feel cornered.

He really didn't know what the hell he'd been playing at. He just knew that he found her physically compelling and that attraction had wreaked havoc with his usual ferocious self-control.

'I could apologise till the end of time but you should know that I find you physically attractive.'

'No! I don't want to hear this!'

'Because it's out of order? Or because you're terrified that it's returned?'

'Gabriel, I don't know what's happened over here…'

'Life got in the way of common sense. Neither of us can take back what has been shared. I want you.'

'You can't say stuff like that.'

'What would you do if I kissed you?'

'I would… I would…'

'Kiss me right back?'

He leant into her and Helen knew what was going to happen next. He was going to kiss her and she wanted him to: wanted that with every ounce of her being; wanted to feel the coolness of his mouth heating her up; wanted to feel his touch rouse her even further. She was so wet for him right now that her mind was alive with images of his hand down there, cupping her wetness, exploring her with his fingers.

She stood on tiptoe, her eyelids fluttering, and put her hand behind his neck to draw him down to her, losing herself in the sweet taste of his mouth as it met hers with a hunger that matched her own.

She stifled a cry of pure, forbidden pleasure.

Their tongues meshed and he propelled her back against the door, breathing hard, his hand contouring her waist and pushing up under her top, finding her breast sheathed in its cotton bra and caressing it until she wanted to wrap her legs around him and have him take her right here, back to the door.

He pushed the bra down, his mouth never leaving hers, found her nipple and she whimpered with uncontrollable pleasure. She wanted nothing more than for his mouth to leave hers, to move to her breasts, to suckle on her nipple.

The knock on the door was so shocking that it took a few seconds to penetrate the haze of lust, but it did, and Helen scrambled back and looked at him with wide, horrified eyes.

Neither said a word and there was another knock, this time a little harder. Gabriel raked his fingers through his hair and stared at her, but then he opened the door a fraction—enough for him to see who was out there and for Helen to hear them. The soft, confused Italian accent apologised for dropping by.

She straightened herself, breathed in deep and stepped around Gabriel, because she couldn't hide in the bathroom, duck under the bed or try an escape route out back.

It was perfectly acceptable for them to be doing some work together. She tried a smile as she met Arturio's gaze, but she could feel red-faced guilt stamped all over her face. She had met him a couple of times. He was as old-fashioned as they came and the look he was giving them both now bore that out.

'Have I interrupted something? Please accept my apologies.'

'Work!' Helen's eyes glassed over. 'It's—great to see you.' She tugged at the tee shirt as she felt the blazing heat in her cheeks.

'You two... My dear, I didn't know.' He turned to Gabriel. 'You should have mentioned that you were going out, Gabriel!'

'We're...we're...' Her voice petered out...

Arturio's surprise had turned to delight: he and Helen had hit it off the first time they'd had met months ago.

She glanced across at Gabriel and he returned her gaze but only briefly, for a few seconds. He knew what she was going to say. The truth—that they weren't going out.

But then, what were they doing? She was in his room and any idiot could see from the flare of hectic colour in her face that, whatever they'd been doing, going over the books hadn't been top of the list.

A little bit of 'hanky-panky'... Arturio would get it. He might be a traditional Italian family man but he was also a man of honour and, if he disapproved of a little bit of 'hanky-panky', then it wouldn't stand in the way of their deal.

Or would it? There was nothing wrong with fooling around between two consenting adults although, frankly, that brief moment hadn't felt like it at all. Not as far as his definition of it went. In fact, several months with his ex had felt more like fooling around than ten seconds with his secretary... What was that all about?

For the first time in his adult life, Gabriel was lost for words. Realisation surged through him with force, a realisation of how much he wanted this old man's approval, of how much he wanted this deal…and of just how much this deal was more than simply the purchase of some vineyards that belonged to a distant relative.

Gabriel had had no contact with any other distant relatives on either of his parents' sides. Only children, both of them and he an only child—their lineage fading away because it hadn't been looked after with love and respect. His self-centred, self-obsessed parents had flown the nest and never looked back. And he had flown even further, leaving America at eleven, by which point he'd had nothing to do with any Italian relatives. He had never given much thought to his relatives in Italy, or anywhere, for that matter.

But then he had decided to expand his vineyards and thoughts of his native land had seeped through his general indifference. He had targeted the region where he had been born. Had that been a subconscious urge to form links with a past he had never known? Maybe. Maybe it had been a whimsical link, but then fate had stepped in, and the link had developed a solidity he could never have predicted.

He liked, respected and admired Arturio. He looked forward to getting to know him better over time. He wanted to meet all those family members, many of whom worked in the vineyards in some capacity or other.

His parents had ditched their past because the present had been way more interesting to them. He wanted to be a different man to them.

Deep inside, he knew that Arturio would be disappointed in a guy who fooled around with his secretary.

Disappointed with a guy who made fooling around with women his stock in trade because he wasn't interested in committing. He shifted uncomfortably as parallels formed in his head, parallels with his parents, who had shunned committing to parenthood just as he shunned committing to anything beyond work and making money.

His priorities were ones that would be alien to the old man looking at him with a question in his eyes.

Helen stared at this big, powerful, self-assured man as he raked his fingers through his hair and struggled to find the right words to say that would somehow rescue the situation from sounding tawdry and distasteful.

She had never seen Gabriel vulnerable before, but he was vulnerable now. Had he ever in his life been at the mercy of his emotions? Standing there, did he even recognise that that was what was happening?

She felt sure Arturio wasn't going to pull out of the deal because he disliked the conduct of the guy buying his vineyards, but something would be lost to Gabriel in the process—perhaps a relationship he had never foreseen but had grown to want, whether he could admit that or not.

Arturio was a passport, of sorts, to the sort of family life he hadn't had, from the little she had read between the lines.

She took a deep breath and smiled at Arturio.

'Yes, Arturio, we're going out.' She smiled. 'We work together, so we haven't been shouting from the rooftops, and it's early days yet.'

She wondered what Gabriel was thinking. Was he shocked? More unexpected behaviour from his predictable secretary! It was oddly gratifying to think that. Besides, the gesture had made her feel pretty good. She would be gone the following day and this inconsequential little white lie would, at least, allow him to follow the path that had unexpectedly opened up to him.

She cherished the bond with her father. She had no idea what life would be like without him and without the various members of her extended family they saw on a regular basis. It touched something in her that Gabriel could be moved by the unexpected family connection he had discovered. It showed a side of him that was poignantly human, a side he guarded so well, despite his apparent openness when it came to his varied and chequered sex life.

She slid a sideways glance at him and then shivered as he reached to rest his hand on her shoulder, a touch that made her body hum in pleasured response.

For just a split second, she wondered whether the recklessness that had been washing over her ever since she had arrived in this magical place was quite as harmless as she'd imagined.

But then she reassured herself that this was just a simple favour she had done. She had grasped the situation and acted accordingly because...because...

Her mind skittered away from the thought that what she felt for her boss might be more than just physical attraction.

It settled on the more harmless conclusion that she had acted like a friend because, after all, weren't they friends at the end of the day? She'd helped him out as a friend.

CHAPTER FIVE

'YOU DIDN'T HAVE to do that…'

They were still standing outside. Arturio had made exclamations of delight, profuse congratulations and a thousand apologies for showing up unannounced but, 'Isabella insisted on spending one night at one of the cottages because they looked so romantic!'. He had now vanished back to whichever cottage they had managed to secure for the night.

Gabriel might have mentioned where he was staying over the phone, when Fifi had made the arrangements, never thinking that a few words thrown into a conversation would have the repercussions that they had.

Now, he stared down at Helen's upturned face, her fine bone structure highlighted by the twinkling fairy lights strung everywhere, which had switched on as the sun had disappeared.

He was disconcerted to think how easily she had read him and how smoothly she had rescued him from a situation he hadn't anticipated. Had she somehow known just how much this whole deal meant to him? How much he had ended up investing in a family he'd previously never given a passing thought to?

Did the woman know him that well?

It was an unsettling thought and he abruptly decided to focus on the basics and not allow his mind to start wandering too far off the lead.

'No, I didn't.'

Then why did you? was the question he fought against asking, because the answer might not be one he wanted to hear. It was one thing to have affairs with women who didn't come close to getting into his head. It was another to look at this woman and realise that she might be the one person who did.

'But thank you for the spontaneous gesture,' he drawled, drawing back slightly. 'The deal isn't signed off yet and we both know how much I'd like to get my hands on that vineyard.' He paused, clenched his jaw and averted his eyes from hers. 'A bonus is definitely on the cards for you, Helen, and it'll be a generous one.'

'That's not why I did it,' Helen said quietly. 'I don't care about getting a bonus.'

'Maybe you were just on a high after what happened between us,' he suggested in a roughened, wicked undertone.

'It's not always about—the physical, Gabriel.'

'I know.' He raked his fingers through his hair and shook his head. 'At any rate,' he said gruffly, 'thank you.' He meant it—and yet he would have rescued the situation somehow. She had cleverly stepped in but he hadn't needed her. 'Need' was not something in his psyche.

He rushed into speech. 'It's getting cold out here. You—you should head in. Last day tomorrow. No need to do anything at all. Enjoy the place. Go into town. Clear your head.'

Helen realised that actually he was the one who needed to clear his head. Hers felt fine. She'd succumbed to the moment and she didn't regret it. A little less comfortable was what she and Gabriel had been doing when they'd been interrupted.

Did she regret that? Since the business with her broken engagement, she'd stuffed her sexuality in a box and pretended that it didn't exist. Working for Gabriel, it had been all the more imperative she never acknowledge what her own body might feel like were it to be aroused because, somewhere at the back of her mind, she accepted that her boss could very well be the guy to show her.

She was so used to caution ruling her life that the very thought of letting herself go to something that was bigger than her was inconceivable. But out here the ground had shifted and she'd opened the door to temptation. She'd let him touch her because she'd wanted it—and she'd rescued him from an awkward situation just then with Arturio because he got to her in all sorts of ways that weren't altogether physical.

He was a physical guy whose brain travelled on a one-way track but that wasn't her.

Confusion and trepidation tore into her. What would he do if he started thinking that she had feelings for him? Did she have feelings for him? She couldn't have. He wasn't her type.

George hadn't worked out but that didn't mean that her choice of guy had been completely off-target. It just meant that youth had stopped her from exploring what else was out there first. She had been conditioned by her over-protective father to gravitate towards safety and she'd jumped in at the deep end without giving it as much thought as she might have. She still wanted someone who believed in love, believed in marriage and wanted security and stability, just as she did.

Gabriel wasn't that man. He was sexy, so she'd been attracted to him. She was only human, after all. She was still young, she was a woman and she decided that, however imprudent her behaviour had been, there was nothing really to be ashamed of. She'd let nature get the better of her for once. And, if she'd been savvy enough to gauge the situation with Arturio and act on it, then it was because it had really been no skin off her nose. Besides, whilst Gabriel might not be her type, she still liked him and could still appreciate those qualities in him that made him a man worthy of respect.

Gabriel, though… Was he torn with guilt? Would he think that she had over-stepped the brief by what she had said to Arturio? Worse, would he get it into his head that she had been expressing some kind of secret desire for them to be an item?

It made her break out in a cold sweat.

She could downplay that bit of it, bury it under the tug of war that had been going on between them on the physical front, he'd get that. For both their sakes, it would work.

'We need to talk this through,' she said firmly. 'Maybe the bar? I could have something to eat. I haven't eaten yet.'

'You want to talk about it?' He sounded startled. 'I didn't think that you were open to discussions about things that happen that shouldn't have happened.' He shot her a wicked, sideways glance. '"Sand" and "ostriches" spring to mind.'

'I know I said before that—yes, okay—what happened a few days ago was a blip that should never be mentioned again. But what happened…' She drew in a deep breath. 'What happened back there was more than a blip…' She shot him a quick glance and gathered her scattered self-control. 'I also don't want you to start taking the blame for anything.'

'Helen, I'm not a fool. I'm a man with a great deal of experience, and of course I hold myself responsible for my shocking lapse in good judgement.'

'Let's just say that it takes two to tango.' She began walking towards the reception area, behind which was the gorgeous bar that gave out to the fields and open land behind, and which was bedecked with lanterns and clusters of sofas, chairs and thoughtfully positioned outdoor heating for when it was a little chilly.

She was so aware of him striding alongside her that it made her body go hot. She thought of them together, and she wanted more, and then she went even hotter when she wondered how long that want had been brewing away under the surface. He would shoulder the blame for what had happened and that said so much about the man that he was. He might pick women up and drop them just as fast but he played fair because, as he had once murmured in passing, he never promised anything. And that was an intensely attractive trait.

'And did you enjoy the tango, Helen?'

'I…' She blushed. 'It happened and…and…'

She shot him a sideways glance as they were ushered to their tables in the bar that, thankfully, was free of Arturio and his wife.

Barely glancing at the menus that were brought for them, she ordered some tapas and a glass of wine, and then sat forward to meet his dark gaze head-on.

From being the dutiful secretary, she felt oddly empowered as their eyes met. Their unusual interlude had altered the balance of their relationship and there was no point trying to unpick the situation. Maybe it was a good thing that he had seen beyond the professionalism to the woman underneath.

He was a guy in the enviable position of being able to have whatever woman he chose, and the women he chose all seemed to be women who would do anything for him. She would just have to make sure he knew that she didn't include herself in that category, whatever had happened between them. She might fancy him, but she hadn't joined his fan club. Things would revert to what they had been once they returned to reality, but he would no longer smile those annoying, amused smiles because she would no longer be the person he'd assumed she was.

'And?' Gabriel prompted, settling into the chair and giving her his undivided attention.

She raised her eyebrows, going for light-hearted and steering clear from serious. Light-hearted was the response of a woman in cool control of a situation, whatever had happened. Shame she didn't quite recognise that version of herself.

'And I don't regret it,' she told him simply. 'Like I told you, I was engaged once, and maybe over here it felt right, even though it was probably a little crazy.' She smiled and kept her cool—just.

'I like a woman who doesn't have regrets.'

'Have you had a lot of experience with ones that do?'

'Enough.' He ran his fingers through his hair and looked at her steadily, seriously. 'But only with women who ended up wanting more than was on the table, than was ever going to be on the table.'

'Like Fifi?'

Gabriel grimaced. 'Correct.'

'What happened there?' She never asked him anything

truly personal, but this was personal, and it felt exciting and alarming to have this conversation.

'Like I said...' his dark eyes were lazy, yet focused '...didn't work out.' He sighed. 'She decided that it might be a good time to explore other options between us— options that might involve rings and jewellery shopping in the not-too-distant future. I was astonished and then I made the mistake of bursting out laughing.'

'Poor woman.'

'Why?'

'She just wanted a serious situation.'

'And she deserves one. Just not with me.' Gabriel paused. 'Although...'

'Although?' Helen broke eye contact, sipped some of the wine and dipped into the tapas which had been brought to them. Her voice was light but she was tense with the realisation of just how far out of both their comfort zones this conversation was taking them.

'Although,' he said smoothly, 'those tapas won't stay hot for ever.'

Helen blinked. He'd closed the conversation and that was a relief, she told herself. Trample over the boundary lines too much, and how on earth would they be able to put them back up? It was a sobering thought. He had come close to saying...what?

She'd told Arturio that she and Gabriel were an item. Had he been about to stress his lack of availability just in case she'd got it into her head that the fiction she'd concocted might turn into reality?

She took a deep breath and decided that she might as well address the elephant in the room and get things back on as even a keel as she could. If he got it into his head that she might become another Fifi—unlikely, but who knew?—then her continued presence around him at work would end up wrecking their working relationship and her job, which she loved and which was so well paid.

'About what I told Arturio…'

'That we were involved in a hot, clandestine affair?'

'That's not what I said.'

'He's traditional and he's a romantic. The family fortune was split several ways when various members died. It wasn't a sprawling family. Arturio got the vineyards, and of course all the land and estates that went with it. My father got the shipping business, which ran itself, and of course coincidentally married a girl whose family fortune made his own pale in comparison. Where Arturio worked from dawn to dusk to make the most of his unpredictable inheritance, my parents washed their hands of Italy and were happy to tour the world and live off an income that dropped into their bank accounts without having to do the graft to put it there.'

'You admire him a lot, don't you?'

'He's more of an example than my own father ever was,' Gabriel admitted. He grinned and looked at her with his head tilted to one side. 'His wife's father worked for him, but he said that it was love at first sight, despite the fact that they came from wildly different backgrounds. Passion, love…heady mix. I fancy that's what's going through his head at the thought of the boss and his secretary—a couple of lovebirds who just couldn't resist the heady mix.'

'That's ridiculous…'

'Who knows what scenarios he's concocting in his head?' Gabriel was still grinning with wicked amusement. 'I don't have a romantic bone in my body, but it doesn't take too much imagination to work out what he must be thinking.'

'Well, he's way off-target with that one,' Helen said briskly.

'Yet you can't blame him. He caught us red-handed, after all. He was probably tickled pink.'

Patches of bright colour stained her cheeks.

'Well, isn't it just as well that I'm leaving to head back to London tomorrow?' she said. She focused on London, the office, his desk, her work outfits—she focused on re-membering that those were the things that mattered. His words were so evocative, made her feel so hot and both-ered. She thought that, however much she made a deal of being in charge of her emotions and in control of what was happening between them, she really lacked the expe-rience to deal with a man like Gabriel. It was important he didn't realise that but it was hard to meet those lazy, penetrating dark eyes without breaking out in nervous perspiration and giving in to the temptation to dab her forehead with the linen napkin by her plate.

'Isn't it?'

The wretched man was still smiling. She cleared her throat and angled her head haughtily. 'I shall head into town first thing. When you see him, you can say that that was always the plan—which it was—and that I wanted to get some last-minute shopping in before I left for the air-port. Because he thinks we're some kind of old-fashioned, romantic couple doesn't mean that he'll expect us to be glued to one another's sides.'

'That might very well be the case.'

'And I just want to say that—being out here—we were in a bubble. When we're back in London, there's no bub-ble and…' she breathed in long and deeply '…I want this to be put behind us.' Her head said this was imperative; everything else said that it was easier said than done.

'Think it's going to be as easy as that?' he said, reading her mind.

'It has to be because, if it isn't, then I'm going to have to hand in my notice and I really love what I do.'

Their eyes met. She sipped her wine and looked at him, her face revealing nothing in the subdued lighting while her heart was beating like a sledgehammer inside her.

Gazing right back at her, Gabriel could only admire her cool.

She'd been swept up by something bigger than both of them, just as he had been, and in that crazy place there had been no room for rational thought.

But that didn't matter.

She'd thrown down the gauntlet—forget this ever happened or she'd quit—and he knew that she meant every word she'd said. When he considered her doing that, he drew a blank.

'Arturio will never be the wiser that we're not a couple,' she said, breaking the silence as he sampled the tapas between them. 'Your deal will go through and at some point when you see him again…'

'Relationships end, and even the die-hard romantic can appreciate that.' Gabriel filled in the blanks and she nodded.

It all made sense and, truth was, he couldn't envisage walking into his office without the expectation of her being there. But forgetting that it had all happened—how easy was it going to be to shut that open door? He still wanted her and she still wanted him. They'd both let the genie out of the bottle.

Yet his hands were tied and that, in itself, was new for him.

'Agreed.' He reached out to shake her hand. 'Back to the status quo in London and picking up where we left off...'

Helen thought she'd handled the situation really well.

The following morning, as she flung the rest of the stuff into her case she had brought with her, she reflected that she had successfully managed to get on the front foot.

Inside? She was all over the place, emotions running high, head filled with questions, doubts and a reckless sense of daring that made her light-headed, frightened but excited, as though one foot was poised, outstretched, taking a different path in her life.

Outside? She was cool, calm, mature and laying down all the rules and boundaries she knew had to be laid down if they were to continue to have any kind of working relationship. Gabriel had crept through a side door and entered her personal life, and she knew that she couldn't allow him to remain there.

When she thought of him, she shivered. He was so wildly different from any image she'd ever had in her had of the perfect guy, and yet so powerful in the position he now occupied. Maybe those snatched moments with him had been important when it came to showing her that the time had come for her to move on with life and start dating again.

Naturally, not with someone like Gabriel, but perhaps someone in between...

Once upon a time, growing up in the shadow of her father's loving anxiety and desperate need to protect her from anything and everything, safety had been paramount. Whilst it was still important, London and working for her charismatic boss had opened her eyes to what adventure might taste like. And, being out here, she had seized the opportunity to go where she had never dared go before.

It had been wise to lay down that ultimatum. It had been clever of her to put up the sort of defence that would protect her from—weakening.

She zipped up her case and for a few moments looked at herself in the full-length mirror, making sure the image would be just right when she next saw her boss. She saw average height, slim build…a coltish figure, which some might like but many might not…with chestnut-brown hair and eyes with just a hint of green.

She'd never given much thought to her looks, and had certainly never considered herself to be anything but averagely attractive, but when Gabriel had touched her she had felt *oh, so sexy*. Even thinking about it now made her shiver.

They had agreed that they would have breakfast together, a perfunctory meeting to go over any final bits of work, and then the rest of the morning would belong to her, with a taxi coming to collect her just after four.

Accordingly, she had dressed for shopping, relaxing and seeing Gabriel in a multi-purpose outfit: light cream trousers, a sensible cotton shirt with a round neck and buttons up the front and her trusty flat shoes. No laptop bag to hide behind, but her backpack and a little nylon bag strapped round her waist for easy access to her phone.

She had no idea how she would feel, seeing him after the night before, but she told herself that it would be a good opportunity to reinforce the message she had sent. He'd always been the one to do the walking away. She knew that. How would he feel now that the shoe was on the other foot? When she thought that he might just see that as a challenge, she shivered with a dangerous mix of dark excitement and thinly suppressed panic. No—it was a definite plus that she had slammed down her boundaries.

She swung into the restaurant, where the buffet was laid out to the left in groaning splendour, cast her eyes around the room, which was filling up, and then abruptly screeched to a halt and stared.

From the opposite side of the room, Gabriel spotted her roughly at the same time as she spotted him, and he read the expression on her face with ease.

Oh no, help...!

He couldn't blame her. Her bright plan to disappear back to London without seeing Arturio was now in tatters because Arturio and Isabella were both right here at the table with him. A pleasant surprise for him, a nasty shock for her.

He waved, rose to his feet and then walked to meet her. It was a nice opportunity to lean into her, a gesture of love and affection, he hoped, because they were in full view of Arturio and Isabella. He whispered into her ear, 'You need to brace yourself.'

'I didn't expect Arturio and his wife to be joining us!'

'Smile and look loving.' He swung round with her, holding her close, but there was no chance to say anything else. 'Remember that we're an item...'

Arturio was already standing. He and Isabella were smiling, and Helen wondered why she suddenly felt a frisson of apprehension trickle through her. The warning 'brace yourself' seemed ominous.

Arturio was a short, plump man with thinning grey

hair and a face that was weathered from the sun and a life lived outdoors. In contrast, his wife was tall, willowy and, for a woman in her seventies, remarkably youthful-looking and rather beautiful, with striking dark eyes and grey hair pulled back in a bun. It was easy to picture the beautiful young girl from the opposite side of the tracks who'd captured his heart.

She had no idea what to expect and was determined to wriggle out of a lengthy breakfast which would be spent pretending to be someone she wasn't, in a relationship that was fictional, even if she had been the one to kick-start the fiction.

She went beetroot-red as Gabriel pulled out a chair for her and simultaneously dropped a kiss on the side of her neck, just a brief, passing caress that feathered on her skin. Just what she didn't need when she had done her utmost to recalibrate their relationship.

Helen hoped for some polite chit-chat and, as soon as she was sitting, said that she couldn't stay.

'I'm leaving later today.' She smiled and eyed Gabriel's hand on the table before reluctantly linking her fingers through his to maintain their charade. 'So, a bit of retail therapy is called for.'

Gabriel squeezed her hand.

'So,' she continued, 'just time for a quick cup of coffee and then I'll be off.' She looked at Gabriel and kept the smile on her face. 'As we, er, discussed last night... darling.'

'We certainly did,' Gabriel agreed warmly.

'How are you both? It's so exciting about this marvellous deal and the fantastic family connection. I know Gabriel will be brilliant when it comes to carrying on the tradition at your lovely vineyards and, of course, expanding and updating a lot of processes, which is what we discussed.'

She was smiling a full-wattage smile, conscious of background noises, the sound of people moving around, eating breakfast, chatting and waiters weaving between tables with trays and pots of coffee. Mostly, though, she was conscious of the Italian couple beaming at the both of them in a way that was vaguely disconcerting.

Her voice petered out but the smile remained in place.

'So…' she said vaguely.

'I don't suppose Gabriel has had a chance to tell you…' Arturio's dark eyes twinkled and his wife leaned forward with a smile.

'Er…?'

'Arturio and I have had wonderful thought,' Isabella said. 'This deal with our vineyards—this wonderful family connection that is already bringing us so much joy… Over the past few months, we've come to see Gabriel as a son as well as a businessman, and to hear that you and Gabriel are going out… We thought it would be lovely if you both came to Italy from here to meet the other members of the family.'

'Sorry?' Helen sat forward, detaching from Gabriel's linked clasp at the same time and shoving her hands on her lap. Her eyes had glazed over.

'We can tell from what Gabriel has told us before you came that what you have is serious—we know that he isn't the sort to get involved with someone working for him unless it is, which we appreciate. We understand more than most how sometimes relationships can overtake common sense and, when that happens, it does no good to wage war on it.'

Helen was straining towards the elderly couple. She

wasn't sure which strand of information was most appalling: an invitation to Italy as the couple they weren't, where they would have to cement their lie yet further; the generosity of Arturio and his wife, who now saw them as part of their own family; or the weight of trust placed in every single word spoken now.

She'd never felt more of a fraud. She'd landed them in this situation. It had never dawned on her that, during the many conversations Gabriel had had with Arturio, he had promoted himself as the sort of guy he knew Arturio would thoroughly approve of. The sort of guy who would never get caught red-handed in a clinch with his secretary just for the fun of it.

She shot them a ghastly smile, stumped for anything to say.

'I have told Arturio,' Gabriel murmured from next to her, 'that you have responsibilities in England which might make it difficult for you to contemplate their kind offer.'

'Yes…'

'Family responsibilities, my dear?' Arturio ordered them all coffee and Helen settled into her chair, deprived of all hope of heading off to town without having to spend time in their company promoting a falsehood she was coming to regret. 'Gabriel mentioned something of that nature.'

Helen looked sideways at the brooding guy sitting next to her and, in silent response, he reached out to squeeze her hand.

'My dad,' she said jerkily, determined at least to be truthful from this point on rather than get mired in yet more falsehoods. Gabriel knew next to nothing about her personal life but, where only a few days ago sharing on this level would have appalled her, it seemed insignificant given the current situation. The rule book had been tossed through the window.

'He lives on his own,' she said. 'Quite far from London. Cornwall, as a matter of fact. I—I try to visit him at least once a month. He worries, you see.'

'I understand.' Isabella patted her hand. 'We parents make a habit of worrying about our children. It is only natural.'

Helen thought of her father—the cards he sent her on a regular basis, the long, casually worded emails that couldn't quite hide his daily anxiety that she was okay, the absolute relief and love on his face whenever she went to visit him. He never *said* anything, but she knew that it had taken a lot of courage for him to let her fly the nest without protest, to understand.

And now here she was, gazing into this lovely woman's concerned face, wondering how she could wriggle out of the situation she and Gabriel had jointly brought on themselves. Well, largely her, if she were completely honest.

'My mum...' her voice was low and quiet '...and my brother died in a car accident when I was very young. My dad never really recovered. He became very protective of me and even now—and I'm twenty-eight years old—he's still very protective, always scared that something's going to happen to me. So I try and get back to see him as often as I can, just to reassure him that everything's all right. It means the world to him.'

'Oh, my dear.' Isabella reached out in a spontaneous gesture of sympathy. 'That poor man, and you, poor child. Of course we must not interrupt that routine! We would so have loved you to have met all our family who work in the vineyards but naturally another time—yes, it was just a spur-of-the-moment invitation. Another time, perhaps, and you must bring your dear father!'

'Yes.' She thought of Gabriel and wondered what this strong, invincible and yet vulnerable guy had said to Arturio in passing when they had met in the past. She thought of the reason why he would have been driven to want the good opinion of someone when, she suspected, he had never cared what anyone thought of him. That one little white lie had now come back to haunt her.

She felt faint. She *did* have feelings for this man. Just acknowledging that fact made her giddy, as though she was at the bottom of the ocean speeding to the surface without sufficient oxygen to take her back to safety.

She'd started this. Might it be up to her to finish it? Would those boundary lines, and her ultimatum about packing in the job if they couldn't put this behind them, still hold up should she spend yet more time in his company? They were finding out about one another and it felt dangerous.

It also made her feel *alive*.

'I'll come. *We'll* come.' She looked at Gabriel and their eyes met, although she couldn't begin to work out what was going through his head. His expression was tender—loving, as a besotted boyfriend's should be—and completely unrevealing.

'I'm not due to visit my dad for another week or so.' She managed a smile as she was swept away on a decision that made her pulses leap. 'And I think he'll like the thought of me seeing a bit of Italy. I haven't travelled much.'

'Are you quite sure, my darling?'

'Yes.' No going back now.

The conversation flowed around her in waves. She was saying stuff but she wasn't sure what. Whenever she glanced down, she saw Gabriel's brown hand on hers, an intimate gesture that reminded her of this unexpected turn they had taken—thanks to her, because he had given her an out clause.

She could have been vague. She could have stuck to what she had said about unavoidable commitments—no one would have questioned that, least of all uber-polite and emotionally generous Arturio and his wife. Maybe she needed this. Maybe she had to address whatever wayward feelings for Gabriel had taken root inside her. Things had become muddled and perhaps she had to wade through the muddle to emerge on the other side and not walk away from it in the hope it would disappear in time.

At any rate, she'd made her bed. She was going to have to lie in it.

'Well, that came as a surprise.'

Helen blinked and realised that Arturio and Isabella had left. She must have said her goodbyes, barely aware of what was going on, her mind way too cluttered with the business of repercussions.

He had dropped her hand and was sitting back in his chair, staring at her.

Gabriel had spotted Arturio and his wife just as soon as he'd entered the restaurant. They'd waved, hurried over to him and, before he'd finished his first cup of coffee, had sprung their idea about a few days in Italy to meet the family.

Gabriel had done well to disguise his shock. He'd

thought of how that suggestion might go down with Helen and come up short, but he'd smiled and murmured something about perhaps her not being able to make it over at such short notice.

They'd wanted them both to fly directly to Italy from America and swing by for a few days—rather as if it was as convenient as stopping on the way from work to buy a pint of milk.

He knew why and had himself to blame. Having spent a lifetime cultivating an armour around his emotions, he had found himself courting the old man's good opinion. Why? Because a door had been opened to what family life looked like? And not just any family life, but his flesh-and-blood family life. Arturio had been cut from such different cloth from that of Gabriel's own irresponsible parents, that he had sought to impress. Having a fling with his secretary didn't come under the heading of making a good impression.

He had been incredibly pleased when Helen had come up with her little fabrication. He hadn't thought that anything further would come of it.

He'd been wrong.

He'd waited for an explosion when the idea had been excitedly mooted, but she'd handled the situation with admirable calm. Definitely not a woman prone to hysteria—admirable, really.

Of course, he could feel her shock and tension in the cool clasp of her fingers dutifully entwined with his, but he'd given her a way out of accepting their offer. He'd opened the door to an excuse involving *family* which was broad enough to include anything: babysitting duties; a favourite cousin's upcoming wedding; a mother in hospital…

The possibilities had been endless.

And at no point had he guessed which road she would travel down. At no point had he contemplated a response that had shocked him, and he certainly hadn't imagined for a passing second that she would actually go and *accept* their offer.

And the crazy thing was that he didn't know which had shocked him more—that sliver of revelation about her personal life or the fact that she'd agreed to go to Italy at the behest of the Italian couple.

'I'm sorry.'

'They can be charming and persuasive.'

'It's only for three days, so I suppose…'

'Helen, this isn't part of the plan for things to revert to normal between us.'

'I know. I couldn't help myself. I like them and I could see how enthusiastic they were to have us over.' There was a lot more she could have said but that would dig deep into personal areas yet again. She decided to stick to vague basics. 'I hated the thought of their disappointment and I hated just—lying more to them.'

'And will you be issuing more threats in due course about moving on, about my mentioning nothing or else you walk? No? Because I made sure to give you a handy excuse for making your apologies.'

He watched as she squirmed, and then he sat forward, leaning into her. His voice seductive, sending little shivers racing through her, he murmured, 'But, seeing that you failed to take up my helpful get-out clause, I think it's time we started finding out a bit more about one another, wouldn't you agree? We wouldn't want Arturio and Isabella to start harbouring shady suspicions about our relationship, would we?'

CHAPTER SIX

HELEN CALLED LUCY. Who else but her best friend would do? The following morning, she and Gabriel would be flying to Italy. She still couldn't believe that she had gone and thrown herself in the deep end when, as Gabriel had calmly pointed out, she had been given a very nice road-map out of the dilemma.

'It's mad,' she said in a hushed, furtive voice as she eyed the bags of purchases Gabriel had informed her she would have to get for their extended trip, and which she had duly bought earlier on company expenses.

Helen had done her training with Lucy and they had remained firm friends ever since. They had both veered off into careers with powerful, wealthy men and mutual venting had been invaluable over the years. Over time two, more PAs had been added to their social media group—Top Secret Secretaries to Billionaire Bosses, as they wryly called themselves—but she and Lucy had their own friendship quite apart from anyone else.

'It's mad,' Lucy agreed.

'I have no idea what happened.'

Helen was not the sort who shared confidences, but with Lucy confidences had been shared over the years, each safe in the knowledge that neither knew each other's boss and so secrets were safe. They trusted one another implicitly. On so many levels, Lucy was the best friend Helen had ever had, so open, straightforward and bubbly.

'It never pays to kiss the boss.'

'Big mistake.'

'But I'm not surprised. You've had a crush on him for a long time.'

'I...' Helen quailed inside. Having a crush on her boss was the last thing she wanted to have confirmed by someone else, and yet of course it made sense, now that her friend had addressed the elephant in the room without bothering to beat about the bush.

Why else did she feel that tingle of forbidden excitement whenever she was in his company? Why else had she postponed getting back into the dating game, even when her head had been telling her that it was time to move on from George? Why else did she never have a problem working stupid hours when he asked her to because some piece of work or other needed to be done faster than yesterday?

A crush that would never come to anything had been safe but taking it to the next level of a kiss no longer felt safe. And she now recognised what she felt for Gabriel was more than a crush but less than...anything dangerous. Surely less than love...? She licked her lips and pushed that thought aside.

'Enjoy the break.'

'Enjoy the break?'

'Well, Italy *is* very beautiful, and I know you've been hankering go there for ages.'

'With Gabriel? In a phoney relationship? Pretending to be someone I'm not in front of people I respect and like, from the little I've seen of them?'

'What other choice do you have at this point?'

'Zero. Why are you always so upbeat?'

'Comes from being one of six kids.' Lucy laughed with just a hint of wistfulness. 'No room to think too much. You just have to always go with the flow or end up being left behind, and sometimes you have to talk louder and faster just to get yourself heard over the din. Remind me to give you the lowdown sometime.

'My advice? My billionaire boss is in a league of his own as well, and has no problem playing by his own rules and to heck with the rest of the world… Take it as it comes and remember that a crush is different from the head-over-heels "in love" thing. Now, the head-over-heels "in love" thing? *That's* dangerous.'

Helen wasn't exactly sure whether she felt better or not after that phone call. There was too much going on to feel anything but low-level panic, which made her think that the best thing she could do was to try really hard not to over-analyse the situation.

When she looked at the brand-new suitcase containing the brand-new outfits for three days of a brand-new *her*, however, her stomach did a few nervous flips and she broke out in a cold sweat.

Because, as well as telling her that she would have to buy some more stuff to tide her through the next three days, Gabriel had also informed her that it might be an idea to think about him when she was choosing what to buy.

'Why would I do that?' Helen had asked, instantly walking into the trap he'd set for her.

'Because,' he had murmured with silky smoothness, 'Bearing in mind you shot down my opporunity to avoid this situation, we're going to have to present a convincing façade to Arturio and his wife and whatever assorted crowd we're going to meet.'

He'd looked at her carefully then, and said in a low, deadly, serious voice, 'This means a lot to me. Not just the deal—buying a vineyard, however much money I make from it, is just something to add to my portfolio. But you can't buy family connections. We are where we are and it's important that we are convincing.'

'I get it, Gabriel,' Helen had said with gruff honesty. She wondered whether he realised just how many inroads had been made into the barriers between them. She thought of his husky, passing confidences, uttered with such sincerity, and her heart clenched.

'He has no idea what sort of clothes your girlfriends like to wear.' She had moved the conversation on, half-smiling, when she remembered the last outfit she had seen Fifi wear to the office—cling-film-fitting hot-pink gym gear, only to be worn by the bold and adventurous, neither of which was Helen.

'Ah.' He had shrugged. 'But *you* know, and it's going to be more convincing if he sees my eyes light up the minute my soul mate and partner walks into the room.'

Their eyes had tangled and for a few seconds Helen had felt the ground unsteady under her feet, but then the moment had passed and normality had been re-established.

They would be flying out together the following morning, arriving only slightly later than Arturio and Isabella, who had already left. They had no idea where exactly they would end up because the vineyards had already been visited and looked at from every angle by Gabriel and his highly experienced team of professionals.

They could have waited but, Gabriel has explained with a shrug, it would be less of an interruption to follow in their wake than if they were to return to London, wait a while and then make the trip over. Helen had seen exactly where he was coming from. If appearances had to be maintained, then there was no point prolonging the situation.

But did he honestly expect her to dress the part of one of his flamboyant girlfriends, when he knew that she was someone who seldom strayed far from sobriety when it came to choosing outfits? He'd really only seen her in work stuff, and here in sensible informal clothes.

So much straying from the norm had happened, though, in the past few days… How did he see her now?

It was an alluring thought—exciting.

He wanted her to "dress the part"—well, why not? That was what had gone through her head when she had sprinted from boutique to boutique, caught up between a sense of cavalier recklessness and the forbidden thrill of wondering whether she was doing the sensible thing. To heck with common sense, for once!

She was less convinced of that particular response now that she was facing the reality of she and Gabriel, and this crazy farce, even though it would only be for a very short while.

There was a knock on the door, and she sprang into action. Gabriel was swinging by for her and they would head to the airport together.

Before pulling open the door, she paused to eye her reflection and was pleased with what gazed back at her. She saw comfortable clothes, but classy with no expense spared, as befitting her new elevation to the role of 'girl-friend of billionaire Gabriel de Luca'—a woman who worked hard but knew how to play as well, and was comfortable in the shiny world of the mega-rich.

A complete transformation. She'd felt guilty at the amount of money she had spent on a few outfits but, then again, playing the part with conviction wasn't going to be a cheap exercise, and she knew him well enough to know that he would be quietly disapproving if she decided to skimp on cost.

He wanted flamboyance? Then he was going to get it. She'd shopped with his reaction in mind. But for the flight over she had gone for cool and elegant in loose linen culottes with a drawstring so that they slipped just a little down her narrow hips, and a sleeveless silk vest, both in shades of cream, and some tan loafers.

Gabriel had stood back and was glancing at his watch when the door was pulled open and, for a few seconds, surprise knocked him for six.

Because this was the first time he had seen his secretary in anything other than what he knew to be off-the-shelf, cheap, cheerful, comfortable clothes for blending into the background. He'd privately always suspected that she scoffed at the sort of expensive designer stuff his girlfriends paraded in. She oozed sophistication, from the willowy lines of her graceful body, to her proud carriage and the way she held herself.

This was a charade, but for a moment it flashed through his head that this was a woman he wanted the world to think was his.

'All packed?' His eyes wanted to linger, to take their time absorbing what they saw.

'And ready to go,' Helen said briskly. She nodded to the two cases on the ground. 'I'm afraid I had to buy a case for the extra wardrobe.'

'You could have bought an army of them if you

wanted.' He swung round and stood aside so that she could brush past him in a waft of highly feminine, floral scent.

Her hair was loose, and the sun and heat seemed to have lightened it. It fell in a shiny, streaky curtain to her shoulders.

'I also have my laptop at the ready,' she said, walking quickly past him and towards the reception area, where she knew their driver would be waiting. 'I thought we might do some work on the trip over. Never mind this deal; I've had a few emails from that construction company poised to start work on the eco-village near Dundee...'

Before the rule book was completely tossed through the window, Helen did her best to remind them both that they worked together—first and foremost, whatever had happened.

Gabriel fell in step alongside her. Dundee... Eco-village... *Right*. That floral scent was penetrating his nostrils, blending with all the other floral scents outside. She was so unbearably fresh, and *pretty*, that it took his breath away.

He dragged his brain back to the present and, for the next couple of hours, managed to immerse himself in the barrage of work-related issues she insisted on dealing with, both on the way to the airport and then, after a brief respite, once they were settled in the first-class compartment of the plane.

'Enough of work,' he ordered when they were cruising and champagne had been brought for them.

He rested one finger on the lid of her laptop and eased it shut. 'I get it that you want to remind me that our peculiar situation doesn't negate the fact that you're still my secretary—and not, as appearances would have it, my girlfriend—but we still have to fill in some blanks before we get to Italy. You never mentioned anything to me about your mother and brother being involved in a fatal car accident—and, first off, I want to say how sorry I am for your father and for everyone else who must have been affected by it.'

Helen's heart sped up.

He hadn't said a word about her outfit, but she'd seen the quick flick of his eyes over her, the way he had quickly lowered them to guard his reaction, and sexual tension had sizzled through her like a live electric charge.

She wanted it and she didn't want it. The conflict inside was sweet torture.

This was all new to her. Life had always been so well organised. This…? She could write off a silly crush, and she could almost shut the lid on those stolen moments between them, when things had got out of hand, because thankfully they had come to their senses. She could very nearly blame it all on being in a bubble, back there in that ridiculously romantic hotel where barriers had been blurred just for a moment.

But now Helen was agonisingly aware that the sand was shifting ever more beneath her feet. She'd felt it before, and the feeling had lodged deep inside, impervious to being dislodged just because she would rather not address it the way it needed to be addressed.

She didn't want some kind of voyage of discovery.

No… She was terrified that part of her wanted it way too much for her own good.

She knew the kind of guy her boss was and she knew that it would be fatal to let herself get sucked into his magnetic orbit. But here they were, and he had a point—they could hardly present themselves as a loved-up couple if a simple question thrown at them at some point in the next couple of days resulted in the whole farce being exposed for what it was.

Her fiancé would know at least one or two basic details about her past! And it wasn't as though she would be divulging some deep, dark, state secrets, even if it might feel a little like that—a little like another chip was being made in the wall she had constructed around herself, the wall that had defined the relationship she had had with him.

'Thank you.' She blinked her way back to the present and to her sexy boss, who was looking at her from under his lush, dark lashes.

'It must have been very hard for you. How old were you at the time?'

'Gabriel…' She turned to look at him, her hazel eyes colliding with his curious, dark gaze. 'I know we have to know a few basic facts and figures about ourselves if we're to be convincing, but honestly, there's no need for detail, is there?' She smiled to temper the cool curtness of her response and hoped he couldn't sense the fear underlying it, fear that her self-control was fraying at the edges.

His eyebrows shot up and he tilted his head to one side. 'I thought what I asked was a basic *facts and figures* question,' he replied. 'So why the secrecy?'

'Because…' She looked at him and sighed. 'I'm your secretary.' She lowered her voice and took a deep breath. 'And not actually your girlfriend, so we don't need to get too much into the details of one another.'

'You know pretty much everything about me. Besides, now that you've invested in this pretend situation, I think it'll work for you to take a little time off from being my employee. Is it really so hard for you to open up a little? You already have. The threshold has been crossed.' His voice was husky. 'I can be a very understanding boss, if you give me the chance.'

The threshold had certainly been crossed, that was for sure.

'Eight.' She looked away and sipped the champagne. 'I was eight at the time. I was at home with my dad, and my mum was with Tommy, who was my kid brother by three years. She was taking him to a birthday party. It was all just—a terrible, tragic freak accident. A pile-up on the motorway. I...' Her eyes glazed over and she drew in a sharp, painful breath.

'You?' Gabriel encouraged gently.

'It was a very bad time,' she confessed, 'if you really want to know.'

'I can only imagine.'

'My dad went to pieces. It took him a while to get out of that black hole but, when he finally did, he'd changed. He wasn't carefree any longer. He became very protective, and I only really noticed it when I got older—when I saw how much freedom other girls had.'

'How did you deal with that?'

'I never minded. I adored my dad and I still do. He was doing his best for me and I always knew that.' She glanced across to him and then laughed self-consciously. 'So, that's my story.'

'Things are falling into place,' Gabriel murmured.

'What is that supposed to mean?'

'Your cautiousness: was George your cautious option?'

'We weren't talking about George.'

'Mistakes get made when you're young,' Gabriel murmured.

'I never said he was a mistake.'

'Despite the painful break-up?'

'Okay, so maybe I played it a little too safe with my ex-fiancé. Maybe we do all make a few youthful mistakes! You must have made some of your own, now that we're sharing our life histories.'

'There are a couple of times I was a bit too impatient in selling shares…'

'I mean it, Gabriel,' she persisted. 'I've opened up, now that we're supposed to be involved and need to know a bit about one another to be convincing. So why should it be a one-way street?'

'If you want to know,' he replied with a thoughtful shrug, 'My parents set a good example when it came to teaching me what sort of mistakes never to make. They were so involved with one another that it was almost like a sickness. The sickness of losing oneself in someone else. So I never made any youthful mistakes. No broken engagements.'

'No broken heart.'

'That won't be my fate.' He frowned and fidgeted.

'You can't be sure about that. No one knows what fate has in store for any of us. Look at the way you and Arturio ended up meeting.'

Gabriel had to concede that she had a point.

'I mean,' she pressed, 'do you really never plan on settling down?'

'No plans at the moment.'

She really wanted to worry this, like a dog with a bone, but did she want to find out more about what made her boss tick? Wasn't that just a road that was going to lead to a life all the more complicated when they were back in London? When they both had to forget this interlude and pick up their normal working life where they had left off? They could step out of their boxes for a while but they would have to keep it light.

'Very wise.' She laughed. 'I don't think all those eligible women out there would ever be able to cope if you weren't on the scene as a prospective boyfriend. What on earth would they aim for?'

Gabriel didn't say anything for a few seconds and, when he did, it was non-committal, amused.

He knew what she was doing, just as he knew that she had felt vulnerable and uncomfortable sharing that snippet of her past with him. But then, despite his invitation to her to ask him whatever she wanted, wouldn't he have walked away from any real personal disclosures? 'Facts and figures', as she'd called it, were very different from the painful business of full disclosure.

He'd told her the truth when it came to his parents. He would never hand his heart over to any woman because he would never risk ending up in a place where uncontrolled passion became the sort of all-consuming fire that ended up burning everything to the ground, from common sense to responsibility.

He was more than happy for sporadic work to be done for the remainder of the flight. When that fizzled out, she read and he snoozed, chair angled back, because it was the only way he could be remotely comfortable, given his size.

They arrived at their destination as evening was falling, bathing the landscape in mellow light.

A chauffeur was waiting for them with a placard with their names on it.

'I don't even know where we're going,' Helen said,

turning to Gabriel as a source of strength as she was bombarded by fast Italian accents and people everywhere.

'"Wait and see", was what Arturio said. Expect many relatives. It's a sprawling family.'

'Maybe that's better than just something small.'

'Less chance for anyone to eke out skeletons in the cupboards, you mean?'

Helen slid a look across at him and felt the tug of familiarity mingled with the excitement of the unknown.

'Something like that. Should we get our stories synchronised?'

Gabriel looked straight at her and grinned.

'It's not going to be an interrogation under a bright light with security at the doors in case we try to flee,' he said drily. 'Vague murmurings should be okay. We just needed to know one or two details about one another, and I think we've covered that.'

'I know Arturio and Isabella like me well enough, but I hope the younger family members—you know—don't find it a little odd that someone like you decides to go for someone like me.' Helen heard her own insecurities bounce around in the silence that followed and Gabriel stopped dead in his tracks and spun to face her.

He curled his fingers round her arms and looked at her with deadly seriousness.

'Where does that come from?'

'Nowhere. It was just a passing remark.'

'"Someone like me"? Someone like you?'

'Gabriel, please,' Helen said with an attempt at laughter. 'You're *you*. You're an eligible bachelor with a roving eye who could have his pick of women. Someone here would surely have spotted you in some tabloid or other with a *Fifi* wrapped round your arm—I'm just saying it might not be quite the easy sell you seem to think it's going to be. No matter; we're where we are and, before you say it, I know that I'm the one who managed to prolong this mess.'

'Run with me on this,' Gabriel murmured, hands still holding her still while people bustled around them on the way to collect bags from carousels. 'Yes, I'm a billionaire, and yes, I suppose there are women who find me attractive...'

'That's something of an understatement. Don't forget, I've worked with you for over three years.'

'My point exactly.'

'Sorry?'

'After a long line of Fifis, after a thousand nights out eating in expensive restaurants and sitting in over-priced front-row seats at theatres—after too many nights to count when boredom started setting in before the bedroom lights were dimmed—I finally discovered that what I wanted was right in front of me.'

'And what was that?' Helen whispered.

'The woman who has been at my side for years, who knows me better than anyone, who's smart and funny and unimpressed by all the things the Fifis of this world are impressed by.'

Silence settled between them.

Helen blinked, caught up in the narrative. For just a second, he was so persuasive that even *she* could believe every word he'd uttered. Of course, it was all a convincing falsehood, and the only reason he had just said what he had was to provide her with a plausible back story for an implausible situation.

She pulled away a bit and he abruptly dropped his hands, although his dark eyes were still riveted to her face.

'Nice one,' she said shakily. 'You're good.'

For a few seconds, Gabriel continued to stare at her in complete silence, then he raked his fingers through his hair and turned away.

'Right—bags, and then onward bound on our little unforeseen adventure.'

Helen wasn't sure whether the smooth ride in the limo was quick or whether she was so submerged in her thoughts that the time flew by.

There was no more conversation with Gabriel, because he spent the time on his phone, having extended conference calls because of his unexpected absence from his office for a couple of days. She zoned out because she was fed up gabbling about work-related issues as a cover to hide her growing apprehension.

Her thoughts made her feel queasy but the scenery rolling past them lulled her.

A thousand shades of green unravelled beneath gentle hills, and there were distant views of white villages clinging to the sides of the hills. The sky was milky-blue. It was like being immersed in a beautiful painting and even the passing of cars on the road couldn't quite detract from that sensation.

She blinked as the limo swerved off the main drag to make its way through lush terrain, and then the rise of white stone carved like a monument against a backdrop of clambering houses, variously painted in pastel shades but all red-roofed and symmetrical, like perfectly shaped boxes.

'My Italian roots stem from these parts.'

It was the first thing Gabriel had said for a while and

now Helen looked at him with interest. He was leaning against the door, sprawled in his seat as he gazed at her.

'Does it feel peculiar?' she asked softly. 'Have you never been tempted to visit?'

'No point,' he replied. 'As you know, my parents emigrated to California to make their base there. They were sent abroad to study when they were young and that seemed to have killed any desire to return to Italy. I imagine they weren't close to Arturio and his clan. Polite contact might have been there at the start, when they first left Italy, but it was frittered away. There was certainly no mention ever made of anyone back here.'

'And you've never been curious?'

'Never. Life's too short to become immersed in a past you never knew. Besides, by the time my parents died,' he went on, 'they had exhausted a substantial amount of their joint inheritance. Because my father took little interest in the day-to-day workings of the various companies, he'd failed to see that many of the old stalwarts had retired and their younger replacement weren't quite as dedicated.'

'What do you mean?'

'I mean, I had to do a hatchet job on the failing arms of the business—get rid of the dross and build it back up before I could even think of doing my own thing. There was no need to go to Italy to oversee any of that because the head offices had long been relocated to New York.'

He looked at her. 'How do you manage to do that?' he murmured.

'Do what?'

'Get me to say things I wouldn't normally say.' His voice was a low, vaguely surprised murmur and his dark gaze was speculative as it rested on her.

Helen shivered and made sure to remind herself that the last thing she needed was a couple of throwaway confidences, dragged out of him because of circumstance, to get her imagining that she meant more to him on any level than what she was—his secretary.

She was also aware that there was a danger of him resenting her over time for knowing more about him than he had ever bargained for.

He pointed ahead of them and she glanced to see that their limo was beginning an ascent through the picturesque town towards a distant and sprawling villa, built along the lines of a castle, all white and grey stone that seemed to spring from the very rock on which it squatted.

'I was under the impression that Arturio and his family couldn't quite afford to modernise the vineyards, hence the sale...' she murmured, awestruck by the villa they were fast approaching.

'A castle takes some upkeep,' Gabriel returned wryly. 'Just between the two of us, there was an informal agreement I made with Arturio, that I would look around the place and see what I could do to save it from falling into more disrepair. It would barely make a dent in my finances. His kids have been after him to sell it for a long time, but the truth is the old man is attached to it— probably more than he should be—and I would want to preserve it.'

'A knight in shining armour—whatever the family connection.'

'Well, as knights in shining armour go, it's nice for me to find a role that I enjoy occupying, considering none of my exes would ever agree with the description.'

He looked at her, brooding and thoughtful. 'And with good reason.'

of the bathrooms on the floor they had been designated—safe in the knowledge that the chance of anyone passing him was remote because the place was vast and their wing seemed empty—he thought back to the moment she had walked into the drawing room.

He'd gone down ahead of her to test the ground and fend off the brunt of the questions about them. It had been easy enough because everyone there was either far too polite and well behaved to display avid curiosity, or else too insecure in their English, preferring to dip in and out of Italian. Besides, they had all clustered around him, eager to fill in the gaps about a relative they had never met. That he had brought a woman with him was less significant.

He was fluent in Italian and was in the middle of an anecdote about his Californian vineyard when he stopped mid-sentence and stared.

He'd told her that, for their charade to pull out all the stops, his eyes would have to to light up when he saw her. He'd made some fatuous remark about her wardrobe, safe in the knowledge that there was no way she could ever break habits of a lifetime and really get into character for the part she was playing. The ground had shifted between them but *that much*? No—no chance.

But that outfit for travel had shown a departure from the expected, and when she'd paused in the doorway of the drawing room…

He groaned now, tugged the tie down and then began getting undressed, switching on the stuttering shower and keeping it cold.

Red…where had *that* come from? She'd been wearing red—a deep, sexy red, modestly covering most of her but cut in ways that showed off her elegant sexiness and revealed just enough of her cleavage to have him desperate to see more.

The colour had complemented her complexion and matched the shade of lip gloss she had chosen to wear. If she'd aimed to garner all his attention, then it had worked perfectly. And he knew that Arturio and Isabella had been looking at him with affectionate approval, because the dark flush slanting his cheekbones and his loss of speech had certainly pointed in the direction of a guy in love. Not true, but what else would they have thought?

And the remainder of the evening had passed in a daze. He'd talked and chatted as normal, autopilot taking over, but his eyes had kept straying to her, taking her in, appreciating every gesture and admiring the way she engaged with people she didn't know from Adam.

She had some Italian, and used the little she knew to draw in the younger contingent, of which there were eight, and laughing with delight, begging them to correct her.

The cold water barely contained a raging libido, and he was glad he'd invested in some very staid pyjamas, because had he done his usual and slept in only his boxers then his erection would have been way too easy to spot for his liking.

'Taking no chances, I see,' he drawled, just as soon as he was in the bedroom and had closed the door behind him.

She'd set up camp on the enormous bed and drawn the curtains around it, with only one side open, so that he could see her safely tucked away with her book in her hand and a tense expression on her face.

'I've put some linen on the *chaise longue*.'

'So I see. I'm not anticipating getting much sleep, if

I'm honest. A hard five-five *chaise longue* isn't going to work wonders for a guy who's six-three.'

'I'm sorry about that,' she said politely, and Gabriel grinned and sauntered towards her. He thought back to the way she'd blushed and sighed when he'd touched her and he thought of how far they had strayed from their normal working relationship. This arrangement made sense but it certainly didn't take into account the vagaries of his imagination. Was her imagination doing loops as well? Or had common sense won out at the end of the day?

'Are you?'

'No.'

'Theoretically, I should get the four-poster with the curtains, considering this little adventure is all of your doing.' Then he laughed at her obvious discomfort and added, placatingly, 'Fortunately you're dealing with a gentleman, and I wouldn't dream of depriving you of your beauty sleep. By the way, you were brilliant tonight. I do believe you charmed your audience.'

Helen was busy wondering how a pair of very sensible navy-blue pyjamas could look so unfairly sexy on a man. She wanted to tear her eyes away but she couldn't. They surreptitiously roved over the way the sleeves were shoved up to reveal the dark hair on his sinewy forearms, and her mind was all of a tizzy, imagining what would be revealed if the drawstring of the bottoms was loosened.

'All in a day's work,' she said, clearing her throat, which was dry. 'If you want to lie in, let me know and I'll make sure I'm out of the room before you.'

'There's no need to be quite so formal, Helen, but, if it helps, I'll be up by five and I'll hit the ground running. If I'm to work on the place, fix it where it's in the process of falling down, then I'll need to get an idea of what work might need doing and start mentally doing some costings. So you can lock the bedroom door behind me and take your time getting ready.'

'Good. Yes.'

'There's a strict itinerary for tomorrow and then we can make noises about going. I haven't quite confirmed how long we can stay here, but Arturio knows it won't be longer than three days.'

'Great.'

'Additionally—and you'll be pleased to hear—there'll be some work to do tomorrow, despite the relaxation criteria laid down. I'll want you to schedule all the details of what might need to be done to this place so that I can put things in place as soon as possible.'

He raked his fingers through his hair and shot her a crooked smile. 'Don't fret, Helen, this will all be over in the blink of an eye, and we'll put the whole episode firmly behind us. Indeed, I'm thinking of flying straight to Hong Kong from here to start talks on a little company I'm thinking of merging with one of my own. By the time I'm back in London, you'll be surprised how all of this, everything, will just become a vague and distant memory…'

Time couldn't pass fast enough, as far as Helen was concerned.

She had no idea what she'd been thinking when she'd recklessly abandoned common sense and chosen a wardrobe to impress. Had she wanted to impress Gabriel—show off her assets?

Of course, she'd seen his eyes widen the evening before when she'd daringly worn red. But if anything he was less touchy-feely than before, now that they were here, and he was true to his word when it came to keeping to his side of the bedroom, as per her instructions.

She'd heard him breathing but the old-fashioned curtains around the four-poster bed had cocooned her from the nerve-racking sight of him on that *chaise longue*. Eventually she'd nodded off and he'd been nowhere in sight when she'd awakened the following morning at a little past eight-thirty.

And then there was work—exploring the vast, old mansion, which showed visible signs of decay; jotting down everything he said in a way that made sense only to her. Arturio was with them the whole time. Then they had lunch with Arturio and Isabella, when they discussed myriad possibilities for the place, including restoring one of the wings as a landmark treasure where visitors could pay to visit and sample authentic Italian cuisine in exclusive, traditional surroundings.

And now...another dinner, yet more people to meet, and another dress she wished she hadn't bought...

Because these outfits made her lose control of her thoughts: made her think of herself as a siren out to seduce her man; made her forget that she was just the secretary obeying an instruction from her boss that appropriate clothing would suit their temporary charade.

She eyed the blue number on the bed with a jaundiced, resigned look. It was a wraparound dress in silk that would fall softly to mid-calf, and in the process expose most of her back. She had felt like a million dollars when she'd tried it on in the boutique and she'd imagined the look on Gabriel's face when he saw her in it.

Now? Not so much. She hadn't bargained on wanting too much when she was in these clothes that made her feel sexy and expensive—too much of those dark eyes on her, too much of his hands on her, too much of everything. The confidences they'd shared had bridged a gap between them and it was hard to look at him and remain detached.

She strolled over and held the dress on its hanger up in front of the floor-to-ceiling mirror by the window, trying to work out whether her breasts would be visible under the thin silk. She was wearing only her cotton underwear and was barefoot—no bra, no shoes, no anything but her panties, and oblivious to everything but what was going on in her head.

She certainly didn't hear the door open, nor was she aware of the man framed in the doorway. She only came to when she heard a voice approaching, saying something from a distance, and when she focused in the mirror there was Gabriel, standing there, and then quickly turning to say something to someone before slipping into the room and firmly closing the door behind him.

She turned around, stared at him and the dress fell to the floor in a swirling pool of blue silk...

Gabriel couldn't breathe.

He leaned against the closed door and couldn't *not* stare because he had never seen anything so damned wonderful in his life.

Her small, high breasts were perfect, tipped with deep-rose nipples, her shoulders were slender and defined and her waist was the span of his hands.

The sun had turned her skin pale gold, but her breasts and belly were paler.

'Helen,' he croaked, wanting to tell her that he had knocked, that the door had been half-open when he'd spotted Arturio. He'd known that it would be bizarre for him to shut it, because it was supposed to be the love nest the engaged couple were sharing. It would be expected that he would be eager to step inside after an hour catching up on work in one of the rooms downstairs, rather than keen to beat a hasty retreat because a conversation with his host was more interesting than the woman waiting inside for him.

Her lips were parted and he propelled himself forward, at once trying to look away whilst simultaneously meet her startled gaze to reassure her that…that…

That what? That he was somehow immune to the vision of beauty standing immobile in front of him?

'My God, you're beautiful,' was what he heard himself saying.

Their eyes tangled as he moved closer to her until he was inches away, until the warmth of her body enveloped him.

He reached to cup her cheek with his hand and then trailed his thumb across it, feeling the smoothness of her skin and the softness of her lower lip.

'I want you,' he said hoarsely. His finger was on the mouth he wanted to cover with his own and his erection was a painful rod of steel pushing against his trousers.

'This is crazy,' Helen whispered.

'I know.'

'But…'

'But…it's a craziness both of us need to get out of our system.' He wasn't going to touch her until she told him he could, but he was going to explode if she didn't. Worse, he would ejaculate in his trousers, and he wouldn't be able to stop himself.

She didn't speak. Instead, she took his hand from her mouth, put it on her breast and sighed as he began to stroke the rubbery stiffness of her nipple.

They were expected for drinks imminently. He'd already been running late when he'd headed up the stairs to quickly get ready and head back down.

To hell with imminent drinks.

He kissed her, plundering her eager mouth with his tongue, caressing her breast even as he eased her back towards the four-poster bed until she buckled against the mattress and tumbled back, landing softly with both her hands spread wide.

Gabriel stared, breathing heavily, looking at her spread in front of him. It was a struggle to undress, but undress he did, unbuttoning his shirt, stripping it off and then following that up with his trousers until, like her, he remained in underwear only.

The boxers bulged with the heavy weight of his erection. He was so turned on...

Was she as turned on as he was?

He stepped between her legs, which were dangling off the side of the bed, reached down to cup his hand between her thighs and felt the tell-tale wetness of a craving that was equal to his.

His dark eyes never left her face.

He balanced on the palm of one hand, resting it flat on the mattress, while he gently eased the other under her panties until he was feeling the slickness of the groove there. He stroked and she squirmed and parted her legs wider, eyelids fluttering shut and colour rushing to her cheeks.

Gabriel was on fire.

He knelt between her legs, tugged the panties off and then rested his hands against the soft skin of her inner thighs so that he could spread them and open her up for his enjoyment, for his feasting.

He buried his head between her legs and breathed her in for a few seconds, and then he nuzzled the soft down before sliding his tongue into her, questing to find the stiffened bud of her clitoris so that he could tease it until she was gasping and desperate for more.

She smelled warm and musky, the smell of lust, passion and need, and it thrilled him more than he was prepared to analyse. He just kept licking, lapping her moistness and turning her on until she could no longer stop the unstoppable.

With a groan, she bucked and spasmed against his mouth, and only when she was utterly spent did he blindly fumble in the wallet that had hit the floor along with the rest of his stuff, extracting the foil packet he always kept there.

Heat was pouring through her body.

She half-opened her eyes and looked at him with glazed fascination.

Had this really happened? She'd been taken out of deep freeze and the burn of desire was tearing into her with devastating force. My goodness, never had she been pleasured in such a way before, feeling the earth swirl around her as she rose higher and higher to come straight into his exploring mouth.

Helen knew that she should have felt some sense of horror at barriers not just crossed, but thoroughly stampeded over, but she didn't. She felt powerful, energised and wildly replete.

She curved against him and her fingers trembled as they skimmed over his hard, muscled body.

'I'm sorry,' she murmured without too much regret in her voice. 'I should have waited, but I just couldn't.'

'Nothing has ever felt sexier,' Gabriel growled. 'Unfortunately, I'm so damned turned on that I don't think it's going to be a slow and lingering journey right now. I just want to feel you around me.'

Helen could think of nothing better. She was dimly aware of him donning protection, giving her body time to calm down a little, because after all this time being touched made her feel as if it was the first time.

He mounted her and entered in one deep thrust, and all those tingling nerve endings that had begun to flatten vibrated back into life and, as he pushed deeper and deeper into her, she could feel herself soaring once again, her whole body climbing up and up to an orgasm that was shattering when it came.

Reality only returned when her sharp, mind-blowing arousal and shattering orgasm ebbed away.

He'd rolled off her and was lying flat on the bed, staring up at the silk canopy above them.

What was he thinking?

Helen wondered whether she should be feeling regretful because she wasn't. She'd invited him to touch her and there wasn't a single part of her that wasn't content with the decision she'd made, even though it went against all common sense. In terms of her position as his secretary, frankly it couldn't have been worse.

She reached to cover herself and he stayed her hand, turning on his side to face her.

'Don't. I like looking at you.'

Helen adjusted her position so that she could likewise look at him.

'I don't think either of us can pretend that this never happened,' she said quietly.

'I feel that would be a tall order.'

'And I accept the consequences because I wanted this as much as you did.'

'The consequences…'

Helen breathed in deeply and her steady gaze didn't waver. It was distracting because he was playing with her hair, stroking it away from her face, and his slumberous eyes were doing all sorts of stupid things to her body and making a mess of her head.

'Where do we go from here? How are we supposed to just pick things up and carry on?' she said. 'I accept that you'll have no choice but to let me go.'

'I'm surprised that you feel you know what's going on in my head.'

'Isn't that what's going on in your head, Gabriel? You play the field with women and, when it's over, it's easy for you to move on because you don't have to carry on seeing them. Well, it's a little different in this case, isn't it? You'll have your error of judgement staring you in the face every day, and it would be unacceptable.'

'Who ever said anything about it being an error of judgement? You act as though this has sprung from thin air, but has it? We've been circling one another for days, chipping away beneath the surface. We've crossed more barriers than I even recognised were in place! And we both know there's been more than than—more than just finding out things about one another we never knew before.'

'I'm your secretary.' Her skin was hot and prickly, her body still tingling from being touched.

'You're a sexy, beautiful, smart woman I wanted to sleep with—who wanted to sleep with me.'

Helen blushed at his description. Smart—yes, she would concede that. But sexy? Beautiful? She'd never thought of herself as either of those things. With every word she could feel herself hurtling deeper and faster into the unknown.

'Just for the record, I still want to sleep with you.'

'Don't say stuff like that,' Helen whispered.

'Why not?' He trailed his fingers beneath her belly button and over the soft, downy hair between her legs, and her breath hitched.

'Because...'

'Do you still want this? Us making love?'

'Don't! I'm trying to be sensible.'

'Have you ever been anything but sensible, Helen? Have you ever dared to take a risk?'

'I...'

'Take this risk. We're here for another day or so. Let's enjoy one another—maybe hang around for a bit longer. I've earned the right to do what I want when it comes to showing up in an office and sitting behind a desk.'

'And when it's time for reality to kick in, Gabriel? To face me across the width of that desk and for things to return to what they used to be? How's that going to be possible?' Her words were a desperate plea.

'Have you thought that getting this thing out of our systems, whatever it is, is the very thing that will make it possible to face one another once, as you say, I'm facing you across the width of my desk?'

'I don't understand.'

'When this fire has burnt out,' Gabriel murmured, his hand drifting to her breast so that he could play with her nipple, which stiffened at his touch, 'What will remain will be fond memories of something that came and went. Who knows? Maybe this has been building between us from day one without either of us paying attention to it. It *is* possible, Helen, for two people to make love, to enjoy one another, to have something of a relationship and still be able to face one another afterwards...'

'You make it sound easy.'

'It's as easy or as difficult as you choose to make it.'

There was a flaw in that logic but Helen was struggling to see it, because his words were as soft and tempting as the darkest, most luscious of chocolate. She *wanted* to believe him because she wasn't ready to say goodbye to this wondrous thing he had stirred in her.

When she thought about the business of walking away—of giving up her job, of never seeing him again, hearing his voice or drinking in the way he smiled, the way he laughed, the way he frowned—she felt physically nauseous.

Was he right? Was this something that had been simmering beneath the surface for a long time, finally released into the open?

If people became lovers, wasn't it still possible to be friends afterwards? If people could get married and have kids and then divorce and end up friends, then of course it was possible!

She needed this. It was safe because she wouldn't be foolish enough to try and build anything from it. Surely she could dump common sense and chasing safety just for a while? She would never be able to give up those fundamental principles that guided her, but she could dare just this once, couldn't she?

And the bottom line was that if working with him proved uncomfortable, because of this, then she could just get another job. Yes, she loved the one she had, but if because of this she no longer did then London was a thriving city and she would soon find something else.

'We should head down,' she said softly, but she was running her hand along his sinewy thigh and curling her own thigh over his, which made him smile slowly and with intent.

'We have a little time to ourselves…'

Helen smiled because, if she was going to succumb to this, then she was going to do it without reservation.

'Think you can be quick?' she asked daringly.

Gabriel drawled, 'Now, that's a challenge I can work at trying to overcome…'

Gabriel watched as their cases were being taken to the chauffeur-driven car waiting for them. For a few seconds, he appreciated the sun on his face, then the sound of voices reminded him that they were on their way.

They had stayed on for an extra day at Arturio's magnificent villa, and he and Helen had actually managed to get work done, as they had catalogued what would need to be done insofar as renovations went.

The more he saw of Arturio and his family, the more important it seemed that he discover more about his own lineage. His parents had dumped their country and severed the bonds that had held them there. It felt important that he not follow in their footsteps now that this door had been opened that led to a family he hadn't known.

All told, everything had worked out perfectly, and that included what had started life as a charade and had morphed into something altogether different.

He spun round, back to the present, and watched with satisfaction as Helen smiled and hugged the elderly couple, her warmth as natural as her gestures of genuine affection.

An extra week in Italy, playing truant for the first time

in his life. In truth, Gabriel hadn't expected his desire to last as long as it had. Or perhaps, he hadn't expected his desire to last this long without showing visible signs of waning.

There was a big difference here. Even when it came to the hottest woman, he knew that his attention span was sorely challenged.

But with Helen? To see was to want and to want was to want more.

Rome, he'd told her...

'We can spend a few days there before we return to the grind in London.'

'I've never been to Rome,' had been her response, to which he had immediately wanted to say that there were a million other cities he could introduce her to, all different but equally captivating.

He'd kept quiet about that, however, because work would beckon in a few days and he wasn't into making promises he couldn't keep. A few days' worth of time out was one thing—but making a list of when those time outs would happen? No way.

He shook hands with Arturio, kissed Isabella on both cheeks and then, when he and Helen were finally in the car slowly driving away from the villa, he turned to her.

'Change of plan.'

'Okay.'

Helen sat back against the door, willed herself to relax and looked at him.

The past few days had been just incredible. She had seen her boss for the man he was underneath—the easy charm beneath the driving ambition and the core of steel.

She had seen him overtaken by desire, had seen him

relaxed and sated and had watched him sleep, his breathing low and even, the years dropping from him in slumber. She had heard him laugh with genuine amusement, and seen how thoughtful he could be as they had gone from room to room in the sprawling villa and he had listened to Arturio and Isabella's concerns as the family finances were laid bare. They had welcomed him into their hearts and trusted him the way they would have trusted their own son.

There were sides to him she had only ever guessed at. The only one thing that remained a steady, beating constant was the acknowledgement that he would very soon call it a day and that she would fall in line and accept the inevitable.

What they had, however wonderful it was for her, was living on borrowed time.

He was looking at her now with something approaching gravity and she was already bracing herself.

'I said that we would go to Rome—'

'Which isn't necessary,' she interjected quickly. 'I do get it that time flies, and there's only so long the office can be left.'

'I happen to have some extremely capable people there who can pick up the slack at a moment's notice.'

Looking at her, Gabriel wondered if this was the reason he felt so comfortable with this woman, why his attention wasn't beginning to wander. Was it because she didn't cling? There was no fear that she would start getting the wrong ideas—ideas about settling down, going to bed with him at her side and waking up with him bringing her a cup of tea. She didn't want to domesticate him.

For a few seconds, he thought of settling down with

her and going to sleep with her just there, within reach. For a few seconds, he accepted that playing the field was no longer how he wanted to spend his time, and Helen…

He felt comfortable with her—frighteningly so.

He frowned.

'At any rate, I've realised that Rome—enjoyable as it is—is painfully crowded during the summer months. Tourists everywhere, swarming like ants over everything.'

'Yes, I suppose so,' Helen agreed with a certain amount of wistfulness in her voice.

'So, instead of Rome, I am proposing somewhere closer to Genoa.'

'Sorry?'

Gabriel patted the space next to him and waited until she had shuffled from where she was sitting and strapped herself into the middle seat next to him, then he reached into his trouser pocket and pulled out a crumpled piece of paper which, as he smoothed it on his thigh, revealed itself to be a map.

'Old-fashioned, I know. Most people open a map on their phone, but for some reason I've always carried this around in my wallet.'

'You have?'

Gabriel shrugged. 'Did you know that once upon a time Genoa was one of the richest cities on the planet? It was because of its port. So many of the wealthy lived there that there was more money than good causes to spend it on. They built houses and mansions, and more houses and more mansions.'

'That'll be interesting.' Helen peered at the map, then she looked at him. 'But I don't understand, Gabriel. Why there?'

'Arturio and Isabella. They've opened my eyes to the

value of the family I never knew through no choice of my own. My parents had no use for blood ties. It's time I corrected that oversight…and it will start with the place they once called home.'

CHAPTER EIGHT

GABRIEL DIDN'T QUITE know when he'd decided to abandon Rome in favour of Genoa, a place that had only existed in his head as where his parents had come from—the birthplace they had jointly vacated in their early teens, first to board at school in America, one in California and the other in New York and then later, when they were married, because they had found it boring and stultifying.

He would never know what might have happened had they come from larger, more united families. Would they have been duty-bound to stay? To supervise fortunes that would have been spread around family members?

'We're not a million miles away from the city,' he said now, 'so it's not as though it's going to be much of a detour—an hour or so. I've booked a hotel in the middle of the city for four nights.'

'Are you sure?'

'What's there to be sure about?'

'Well—retracing your past. Wouldn't you rather do that on your own?'

Gabriel flushed. 'That's over-romanticising the situation, Helen. I'm not embarking on a touching voyage of discovery, and I won't be investing time working out the family tree. That said, since when is it ever too late to be curious? We're reasonably close, location wise, and so why not? I've been to Rome a hundred times. If you'd rather I take you to Rome, or anywhere else for that matter, then of course…' His eyes darkened as he brought this back to a level he found comfortable. 'Your body would turn me on wherever we choose to go.'

'Don't be silly.' Helen smiled but her eyes remained serious.

'Like I said, I'm curious,' Gabriel conceded with a shrug. 'Neither of my parents spoke much about the city that had raised them and, when they did, they were hardly flattering.'

'What do you mean?'

'Dull, antiquated, no fun at all… My parents placed a lot of value on having fun which is probably why they relinquished responsibility for me to people they could pay. I don't believe they thought a kid was much fun, far less a baby.'

When she looked at him, he threw her a crooked smile but his eyes were thoughtful. 'You make a ridiculously good listener,' he said gruffly.

'Surprisingly, so do you.' Helen blushed.

'I'll take that as a compliment.'

'You're very spoiled when it comes to women complimenting you, aren't you?'

'Is that because I'm amazing?' He grinned but his eyes remained thoughtful.

'In a way, I guess I could have done with a less devoted father,' Helen said slowly. 'The older I got, the more I understood why he was as protective as he was, but looking back?' She sighed. 'I drifted into that engagement with George because I suppose I was conditioned to be safe, and that was a safe relationship, a known quantity.

It just wasn't the right relationship for me. I guess George drifted into it as well, if not for the same reasons. I guess he found it comfortable, and sometimes men can end up going down the road of least resistance.'

'And here you are now,' Gabriel drawled. 'Burning up the rulebook when it comes to safety.'

'Yes.' But then, she thought in confusion, why did he make her feel so safe if he was so emotionally dangerous for her?

'I can't believe you weren't just a little bit tempted to visit your roots before.' Curiosity brought her back to the topic they had started off discussing.

She thought about what he had said about her being a good listener and it warmed her inside, yet wasn't this a very special trait born from the fact that they had known one another for some time before becoming lovers? Wasn't there a familiarity there that had expanded now that the boundaries between them had become blurred? It was something neither of them had factored in, but it was why things felt so right between them for her, even though what they were doing was so foolhardy.

'It would have been out of my way,' Gabriel said prosaically. 'Now, though? I had no idea Arturio's place was within spitting distance, so to speak.'

'How do you think you're going to feel?'

'Not following you.'

'I mean…' Their eyes tangled and Helen reddened. At what point did she start overstepping the mark? At what point would his shutters come down because, no matter how cosy they got with one another, he would always have a wall up when it came to getting *too* cosy?

'Don't worry,' he said drily. 'You don't have to stock

up on the tissues because there's a chance I'm going to break down and start crying.'

'No, I can't imagine you doing that…'

'And for the record? I've never appreciated girlfriends who go down the psychoanalysing route.'

'But I'm not a *girlfriend*, am I?'

'Touché.'

Helen reddened and wondered, if she wasn't a girl-friend, then what was she exactly? A temporary play-thing? That didn't feel good, but wasn't it a role she had volunteered for? She'd known from the start that he didn't do love, just as she'd known that that was what she wanted from any relationship. But things were changing for her and she was slowly starting to realise how much he could hurt her, how much *this* could hurt her.

'Does X mark the spot on the map?' She abruptly changed the subject.

Gabriel was silent for a few seconds. He thought of that map. It had been given to him by his father years ago. It had been a rare occasion when his parents had been around for a sustained period, something like three months, and he had seen more of them than he ever had before.

He must have been not quite a teenager, before he had begun closing down, forming hard and fast judgements on the nature of relationships that were so all-consuming they left no room for anything else. Before he had begun build-ing his life along the lines of one where control would al-ways trump spontaneity.

He could remember his father trailing his finger over the little icons, chatting about things in the city, the sights and landmarks there. They had both come from sufficient wealth that they'd individually been raised in small palaces although, he had confided to Gabriel, ruffling his hair, his mother had come with the bigger bag of gold.

'There are no spots marked,' he said, withdrawing, because it suddenly felt safer. 'But, I assure you, there will be many things of interest to see.'

'Including where your parents lived?'

'Let's ditch the questions,' Gabriel said softly. 'They bore me. Look at the scenery instead. It's incomparable.'

Helen recognised this for what it was—she was being reminded of her place.

As she gazed out, however, she saw the scenery was as incomparable as he'd said and he relaxed and became an informative guide, pointing out all sorts of things and filling her head with so many pieces of information about the country that she wondered whether he'd made it his mission to read up all about the place his parents had decided to leave behind.

Sepia fortresses rubbed shoulders with clusters of brightly coloured houses, and everything seemed to be embedded into the terrain, a wonderful mix of earthy tones mixed with the greens, greys and blues of undulating hills.

The car weaved through villages and towns at a leisurely pace. Inside it was cool from the air-conditioning but it was easy to feel the heat blasting down from cloudless blue skies. The sea was a constant presence, although it was hard to get a feel for how close or far away they were from it at any given time.

There was a sense of cliffs plunging into ocean, glimpsed here and there as they took a corner, and of entire villages clinging precariously to them, although they were surely in no imminent danger of erosion, because they all looked as though they'd been perched on the same spot for centuries.

She wanted to ask him how he felt, being here, even if he wasn't familiar with the place, but she'd been warned off and she knew how to recognise those boundary lines.

Watching her as she gazed in rapt appreciation out of the window, Gabriel was filled with a sense of well-being.

He actually hadn't got such a kick from sealing any deal in a long time. He was glad that he had branched out to make his own fortune, independent of the wealth he had inherited from his parents, which had still been considerable, even though much diminished from years of profligate spending. But nothing had felt as risky as opening up to Arturio and recognising family members he hadn't even known existed.

And his secretary had been with him for the ride from the very beginning. He'd told her that she was a good listener, and he'd meant it, and when he looked back to before they had become lovers he could see that he'd always found her relaxing to talk to. She didn't demand. She didn't nag. In return, he confided. It was a trade-off that had happened without him even really noticing.

He was looking forward to watching her various expressions of delight at the hotel he had chosen, for once doing his own legwork and sourcing somewhere suitably lavish, not to mention the various places they would visit during their brief stay.

He'd mentally made a list. He wondered what, if anything, she had seen of the world. Her father had been protective, but surely she would have done some travelling, if only to safe, touristy destinations?

'I know your engagement was broken off but where had you planned on going on honeymoon?' he asked curiously, and Helen dragged her attention away from the passing panorama to look at him.

'Nowhere.'

Gabriel's eyebrows shot up in surprise. 'Is that normal? I thought every young married couple was eager to make elaborate plans about where they would go on their honeymoon. The one time to throw financial caution to the winds!'

Helen reddened and she sighed.

'We thought it was more sensible to put the money aside to buy somewhere.' Of course, warning bells should have rung for her at the time for that very reason, she thought. She looked at Gabriel from under her lashes and thought that, for someone who wasn't interested in meaningful relationships, he was pretty emotionally shrewd.

'Don't forget that I was conditioned to be sensible, and maybe George simply fell into line because he was so mild mannered and really quite sensible as well. We both thought buying a house made more sense than frittering away what savings we had on going abroad for a fortnight in the sun. My dad couldn't afford to give that to us as a wedding present, not when he'd paid for the wedding, and George's parents were no better off financially.'

'You must have been very hurt when it all came crashing down.'

'I dealt with it.'

'With your usual cool? Sensible to the end?'

'If I were as sensible as you think, I wouldn't be here.'

'Very, very glad you realise that sensible only works if

you dump it now and again.' Gabriel smiled, eyes darkening. 'Light and shade and so forth.'

He looked at her pensively, watching her blushing smile.

'And speaking of honeymoons...' she raised her eyebrows '...can I ask how it is that *you* never had one?'

'Interesting question.'

'Is that your way of saying that you're not going to give me an answer?'

'Does anyone know me better than you?'

'You're impossible.'

'Is that why you find me so sexy?' He enjoyed the way she went bright red at that—very satisfactory indeed.

'Impossible, and with an ego the size of a cruise liner.' She suddenly wanted him to touch her so badly that it was an effort not to fling herself on his lap and beg him to do with her as he wanted. Thank goodness the privacy partition was shut so that their driver couldn't hear the conversation although, if he glanced in the rear-view mirror, he would easily be able to see the deepening flush of a woman in the grip of lust.

Gabriel was looking at her lazily, reading the mood, which only added to the electrifying charge in the air.

He reached to slide across the screen so that the driver now could neither hear nor see them.

'What would you like to know?'

Somehow, the distance between them had closed. Had he shifted over to her? Had she moved towards him? Or maybe whatever charge had been released had just drawn them together.

'How is it that a guy like you isn't married?'

'Because a guy like me never had any interest in settling down.'

He slipped his hand underneath the knee-length skirt
she was wearing, ran it up her thigh and then, eyes still
pinned to her face, casually pushed his fingers under the
crotch of her knickers, which were damp.

'You think too much about sex…' Helen breathed, her
eyelids fluttering, and Gabriel laughed under his breath.

'Are you telling me you'd rather I wasn't doing what
I'm doing?'

'This isn't—appropriate. Oh…'

'Shh…too much talking. We can return to the tedious
honeymoon conversation just as soon as I've done this…'

He had managed to shove the crotch of the panties to one
side so that he could explore her wetness, and this he did,
fingers inserting deep inside her as she wriggled a little
lower to accommodate them.

Outside, the scenery continued to flash past, a whirl
of various shades of green, hills and mountains rising
and falling, winding roads and clambering villages. All
a background blur to the far more captivating sight of a
woman in the throes of passion.

Her eyes were shut, her lips parted and her shiny, well-
behaved hair was ruffled. Hectic colour was spread across
her cheekbones and her breathing was soft and jerky, the
breathing of someone who wanted to groan aloud but
couldn't.

He could have watched her for ever.

He found the bud of her clitoris and stroked it, and
nearly groaned out loud himself as she slid just a tiny bit
further down.

He watched as she spasmed into orgasm, watched her

colour deepen and her nostrils flare and the bumpy arch of her body, which she couldn't control.

There was privacy glass on the windows but even so the brightness of the sunlight pouring into the back seat of the car left nothing to the imagination.

This was passion at its most powerful and he wished, for a split second, that he could capture it for ever in his head, never to let it go, never to allow it to be become diluted over time.

'There now,' he murmured in a shaky, husky voice. 'Don't you feel a lot better after that?' He removed his hand, which smelled of her musky fragrance, and neatened her skirt.

Helen shuffled back into something resembling an upright position.

She'd never done anything like this in her life before, but then there was so much she'd done with this man that she'd never done before.

And every experience was backlit with something wild, soft, powerful and tender.

She looked at him, eyes widening, and then just as quickly she looked away, but her heart was beating madly inside her.

How had things crept up on her like this? How had she found herself accepting the cards that had been dealt whilst desperately longing for them to be shuffled and re-dealt? He had got under her skin in ways that had been small and subtle but devastatingly significant.

And of course, she had noticed it. She wasn't a fool. She'd known that she was developing feelings for him, but it had been convenient to pretend that she could control those feelings and make sure they stuck to the plan.

If she didn't actually give those feelings a *name*, if she didn't call it *love*, then she could tell herself that she was still in control, even when she felt out of her depth.

She'd done a good job at trying to kid herself.

He touched her and she went up in flames but, oh, it was so much worse than that. He smiled and her heart skipped a beat. He looked and she wanted to faint. He talked and she yearned for him to talk some more, to tell her what she wanted to hear—that he had feelings for her too. That this was more than just a dalliance that had happened out of the blue and taken wings because of circumstances neither of them could have predicted.

She'd been brought up never to take risks and, whilst she had felt protected by that mantra, she had failed to recognise how vulnerable it had left her—vulnerable to a guy like Gabriel, who was so far removed from anyone she could ever have imagined getting to her.

She was in love with the guy and as she sat, mouth dry, thoughts in a panic, she didn't know what to do with that.

She surfaced to find that they were nearing the small town where they would spend the next few days. Not actually in the city, as it happened, but in one of the picturesque little towns close to it, a base from which they could discover the city and its surrounds.

'You okay?'

Helen met Gabriel's confident, amused grin with a watery smile of her own.

'Perfect.' She aimed for crisp and light. She ended up with something of a sickly croak.

'Is it the drive?'

'Huh?' He had the deepest, darkest eyes, Helen though as she stared back at him. A person could drown in them. As she had—she and a million others.

'Some people can get travel sick.'

'Yes.' Helen clung to that excuse with the tenacity of a drowning person hanging onto an unexpected piece of passing driftwood. 'It's—it's my inner ear. It's always given me problems ever since I was a kid. Long drives, planes, boats and stuff.'

'I didn't think you'd done a lot of travelling,' Gabriel said with a frown.

'By car,' Helen answered quickly. 'Cornwall is far from everywhere.' She laughed weakly. 'Even going for a weekly shop could involve miles and miles of, um, travel sickness in my dad's car.'

'Must have been uncomfortable. And I suppose our little bout of activity didn't help matters…' He sent her a wolfish smile that made her toes curl and she heard herself mutter something and nothing before launching into a series of frantic questions about the area. At least when his attention was somewhere other than lasered to her face she could begin to get her thoughts in order.

What was she going to do? How could she have been so smug as to think that she could do as she wished without being affected? How could she have simultaneously spotted warning signs of emotional attachment while failing to take any safety measures to protect herself, to safeguard her heart?

She thought back to the way she had opened up to him, gone from zero to full-blown rocket speed, in no time at all. A little sharing because they had got themselves in a charade; a few confidences so that they could pull off a relationship that wasn't there; then a few more…and now? Now every bit of her had blossomed and opened up, and she was as raw and helpless as a snail without its shell.

And Gabriel? Yes, he had shared stuff with her too,

*but he hadn't given any more than he could get back;
hadn't gone and given her his heart while she had thrown
hers at him, knowing he wasn't going to catch it and take
care of it.*

She was here for a just a couple more days and then
they would return to England.

What next after that?

It was a blessing that he had no idea how she felt.
She'd always been his calm, unflappable secretary and
this arrangement, in his eyes, didn't change who she was.
She was still calm. Not someone who was going to make
waves that would require her dismissal, as had happened
with Fifi.

She wasn't going to make waves now, she decided. She
wasn't going to ask questions that couldn't be answered,
and she wasn't going to give him any indication that she
might want more than what they were enjoying.

For Gabriel, it was all about the sex, whatever personal snippets he had shared with her. He had confided,
and she had absorbed those little confidences, and they
had buried deep inside her and fed her feelings for him.
She had confided and he had responded because he was
interested and because they were lovers, but they hadn't
fed anything in him, because there was nothing to feed.

And, if this was all the time left to her, then why
shouldn't she enjoy it as well? Why shouldn't she feel
like a woman. It had been so long since she had, and a
few more days of stolen pleasure wasn't going to add to
the pain. She was going to hurt, whatever happened.

When they returned to London, she would put a smile
on her face and she would begin hunting around for something else. Maybe she would return to Cornwall. She could

easily use that as an excuse if she wanted to avoid curious questions and raised eyebrows.

He was good at those two things.

'But it was very nice all the same,' she said weakly and he grinned.

'That's sounds a lot like me being damned with faint praise.'

'There goes your ego again,' Helen murmured, more in truth than jest, and he caught her eye and laughed.

'No one talks to me like that.'

'Maybe that's your problem,' she said drily.

'Who knows? You could have a point.'

She said what she thought. She always had. If she disagreed with him over something, or had a viewpoint that didn't coincide with his, she was never shy about telling him and she never feared the consequences.

He'd vaguely thought that that was because she was secure in her job, and knew he wasn't a guy who sacked anyone for a viewpoint, even though not many of his employees ever disagreed with his decisions. He'd also vaguely assumed that, because they weren't lovers, she wasn't in the same bracket as other women who tiptoed around him and were always eager to please.

But now they were lovers and she still didn't tiptoe around him. She *still* spoke her mind. She was still the same cool, composed woman.

Except, underneath there was a depth he hadn't seen before. She'd been hurt by what she'd experienced, and she'd grown from it. She had learned, as he had, that self-control was a good thing. They had both been formed from their backgrounds in different ways. Like him, she knew that life wasn't always straightforward.

His thoughts were running away at a tangent and as the grand, sepia-coloured hotel loomed ahead of them, uniformed attendants waiting to gather their luggage and usher them in, he decided that this had certainly turned out to be one of the best unexpected situations that had happened to him in a very long time.

He was going to enjoy playing tour guide for the next four days.

And he was going to enjoy so much more than that.

Helen looked at Gabriel, seeing him sprawled on the king-sized bed in the reflection of the mirror where she was sitting, brushing her hair.

The sheet was draped over him, just about covering the part of him he had only just very effectively used to bring her to a shuddering orgasm.

He'd offered to run a bath for her, when eventually she had found the energy to move, but she'd laughed and told him that a girl needed a bit of time to herself now and again.

So she'd had her bath, taking her time, and thought about how one pretence had led to another. Pretending to be an item had morphed seamlessly into pretending not to have feelings for him.

This was going to be their last night here. The past few days had been momentous. Today, in particular, her heart had clenched with love and empathy, for he had taken her to see the palace where his mother had grown up.

It had been sold many years previously and had been turned into exquisite apartments. The façade had remained the same, though, and, although he'd told her that it was a modest enough palace, it had still seemed vast to Helen, who couldn't conceive ever living in a place like that.

Sitting with strong coffee in one of the squares, people-watching, she had asked him questions and he had answered without his customary wariness, staring off into the distance, his voice low and thoughtful.

He spoke about his past the way someone might talk about a country they had once visited. Only once had she heard a curious hitch in his voice, a sign that underneath the cool exterior was an undercurrent of emotion of which, she suspected, even he was unaware. She had seen how momentous it had been for him to meet Arturio—life-changing, even if he might not have admitted it.

Helen had wondered whether this was what had sucked her in—a glimpse of someone powerful and impregnable who, without realising it, was also vulnerable and touchingly *human*.

'Penny for them.'

'Huh?'

'Your thoughts. Or I'm prepared to go higher if you'd like more. A pound, maybe?'

Helen laughed and swivelled round on the chair so that she was facing him.

'Much as I enjoy watching you brush your hair, I'd quite like it if you did it in the buff.'

'You can't always get what you want.'

'I've always been interested in challenging that particular theory. Tell me what was going through your head. You looked very thoughtful.'

'I was thinking that we leave tomorrow.'

'Has this part of the world lived up to expectations?'

His voice was still light but Helen felt that she could

hear a very slight shift in it, so slight that it was barely noticeable, but she knew him well—well enough to know that he was waiting for her response, waiting to see what came after that remark.

He would always be the guy on guard for the clingy woman, the woman trying to pin him down and to make more of something than he was prepared to tolerate.

Even with her, even with someone he read as being as detached as he was from any emotional involvement, he *still* didn't quite trust her to obey the rules he laid down.

For a second she wondered what he would do if she confessed everything to him. How would he react? He would be appalled, and would see it as a betrayal of their understanding. When she thought of how his face would change, how he would begin to back-pedal, how that lasting memory of her would be one of shock and dismay, she felt sick.

She would never allow that to happen. She would always make sure that she exited without falling flat on her face in front of him.

'It has.' Helen's voice was normal when she answered and she gracefully rose from the chair to make her way to the wardrobe, from which she extracted what she would be wearing for their final meal in Italy. It was a soft, silk dress with a scooped neck in shades of rich blues and greys. It was very elegant and had cost the earth.

She could feel his dark eyes on her as she eased it over her head, over the bra and panties she had been wearing as she'd brushed her hair.

'It's a beautiful part of the world, Gabriel. There must be a part of you that wishes you could have spent more time here, growing up.'

'If wishes were horses...' But he grinned. 'And you

still haven't told me what you were thinking when you said that this was our last evening here.'

'I was thinking that we've somehow managed to get very little work done, so there's going to be a lot of catching up when we get back to London.'

'And are you looking forward to that?'

'Catching up on tons of work?' Helen grimaced, scooped her sandals up with one hand and returned to the chair to slip them on; the straps were thin and fiddly. 'Does anyone look forward to catching up on tons of work?'

'You've never had a problem with tons of work.'

'That's true.' What a fool she'd been, slowly falling for this guy, never questioning the tons of work she'd always enjoyed doing, even when it had meant sacrificing a weekend. 'Actually,' she said slowly, 'I'm thinking that when I get back I might just take a week out to go visit my dad. Of course, I'll make sure whatever urgent work matters need doing get done before I go...'

She glanced up from fiddling with the straps to find him looking at her with a shuttered, thoughtful expression.

He'd asked her what she'd been thinking. What was going through his head now? Was he going to make a speech about the routine they would get back to once normal life recommenced? Was he going to tactfully remind her that this was temporary, so she shouldn't expect it to carry on once they were back in London?

'This has been pretty intense,' she said seriously. 'There's no question it has to end once we're back in London but, realistically, we might both need a little time out before we face one another in your office. Don't you agree?'

* * *

Gabriel didn't say anything for a while.

His dark eyes drifted over her. She was saying all the right things, and he couldn't help but think about where all that common sense went the minute they were in the sack. When he thought of the way he could consign that practical side of her to a bonfire just by touching her, he felt himself getting turned on.

She did the same to him.

He was as cool and detached as she was—more so, if anything, because there was a sentimental side to her that he lacked—and yet she could rouse him with a look.

'What I'm going to say, Helen, is going to come as something of a shock...'

In a way, a shock to him as well. But things had changed. Fifi had showed up, and everything that went with her, from the demands for more than he could give to the tantrum and the flouncing out. It had made him think long and hard about the future of his choices. Then along had come Helen, as soothing as Fifi had been hysterical, competent and controlled...and, as the days unravelled, unbearably sexy.

Throw Arturio into the mix, along with a vision of family life he had never given passing thought to—and, to that mix, add this visit to Genoa, where he had felt the punch of what he had missed out on from the day he'd been born; the wrenching regret of a palace he had never occupied and the sound of family voices he had never had...

A revolution had been quietly happening inside him, and now...

Gabriel slung his legs over the side of the bed and stood up, unashamed of his nakedness although, as an afterthought, he looked around him, found his boxers and stuck them on before sauntering towards her, only pausing to drag up one of the chairs by the window to join her where she was sitting.

'What is it?'

'I'm asking you to marry me.'

CHAPTER NINE

HELEN STARED AT him in utter silence. Had she misheard? Had he just asked her to *marry him*?

She felt a slow, steady soaring inside her. She'd fallen for this guy hook, line and sinker. What had started life as an impossible, barely recognisable crush had grown at supersonic speed into something deep, powerful and overwhelming.

Looking back, she could see that love had been stirring inside her for a long time until, with circumstances changing the dynamic, things that she had bottled up had been given room to breathe.

Had it been the same for him?

He'd always had such a colourful love life but, underneath it all, had he too been drawn to her? Had love been building up for him as well until, as with her, it had surfaced and knocked him for six?

She blinked.

'Sorry?' she finally said faintly.

She teetered towards the nearest chair and fell into it, but she couldn't peel her eyes from him as her mind played with a series of lightning-fast thoughts, thoughts that were linking up and leading down all sorts of wonderful roads.

'I've never thought about proposing to anyone,' Gabriel

said slowly. He stared off into the distance for a couple of seconds but then he was looking at her again. 'My parents...' He shook his head and shot her a rueful, crooked smile. 'Well, you know from what I've said to you that they weren't exactly the finest example of a responsible married couple with a child to consider.'

'I know they sent you off to board at a very young age,' Helen said softly. 'Maybe they lacked any examples of what responsible parenting looked like, if they were both the products of only children themselves and, like you, were dispatched to school when they were too young to really deal with it.'

Gabriel shrugged. 'I don't deal in the whys and wherefores. I prefer to look at the end result and the end result was an important learning curve for me.'

Helen nodded. She wasn't going to rush this. If dreams came true, then she wanted to savour the journey getting there, getting to the place where the first brick in the wall of happy-ever-after would be put in place. It had been a long time coming and she couldn't think of anyone she would rather spend the rest of her life with than this man sitting so close to her, his dark eyes so serious and focused.

It was a crazy thought, and yet it just felt right.

'Love? Wild, edge-of-seat, reckless love? Not for me. I lived through what the outcome of love like that could be and I wouldn't wish it on anyone.'

'Well...'

'So, proposing to any woman, signing up to having kids? Not a route I'd ever considered. But when I'm with you, Helen, I see a union that could work.'

'A union that could work?'

Something in this speech was beginning to make her

feel a little uneasy. She had predicted where it would go. Her mind had gone hell for leather towards a future sun-filled and alive with possibility. If there was a similar heady excitement racing through him, then he was doing an excellent job of hiding it. He looked…serious and prag-matic.

'We've always got along. That I've known, but until our relationship developed into something else, well, I've come to realise that we're compatible in many more ways. Wouldn't you agree?'

'The sex is certainly nice,' Helen averred, clearing her throat.

Gabriel grinned. 'I feel I may be growing accustomed to your mastery of understatement. Fact is, being with you has shown me that there's an alternative to a tire-some parade of women, all eager to please and in the end—and I hate to say this—all disposable. I'll be hon-est, Fifi kick-started that particular line of dissatisfaction. That she wanted the whole package deal was ridiculous, but really, why? Why should the whole package deal be ridiculous? Yes, with Fifi it was, but with you? You came here and showed me that you fill gaps I never understood needed filling: compatibility; genuine friendship; no de-mands for emotional highs.'

'Disposable?'

'I don't miss any of them when my relationship with them comes to an end, nor have I ever questioned the busi-ness of simply moving on with someone else. It always seemed the only alternative to sticking with one woman and going down the marriage route which, like I've said, was off-limits for me.'

'Because you never found the right woman to love…?'

'Love isn't something I'm drawn to try out for size,'

Gabriel said honestly. 'But until this—this thing that's evolved between us—I've never understood that there's a road between the two.'

'A road between the two?' Her head was swimming. It felt as though she'd started out on a straightforward merry-go-round ride, holding hands with the guy she'd fallen for, only to discover very quickly that after the merry-go-round came the ghost train and the guy she'd been holding hands with had disappeared just when she'd banked on him being there next to her.

It was disorienting, yet she kept a smile on her face while her mind continued to whirl.

She would have liked to place her hand firmly over that beautiful mouth but she also knew that she had to hear what he was going to say until there was nothing left to hear.

'There's no chaos with you,' he said simply. 'By which I mean, we're both on the same page. You don't do hysterics. You take me for the man I am, and you don't want to turn me into a man I will never be.' His voice was low, persuasive and thoughtful. 'I can see life with you because we complement one another, no questions asked.'

'So what you're saying is that we could get married and it would be a bit like a—business arrangement? One where all the right boxes get ticked and so it makes sense?'

'That makes it sound a whole lot less—hot than it is.' Gabriel's voice roughened and the vision of the sexuality between them charged the air with sudden electricity.

In a heartbeat, Helen knew where he was coming from. He had been hurt by his parents and had come to see them as an example of what love could do to a person, how it could consume and take over until two people got lost in one another to the exclusion of everyone else.

He'd been young when those impressions had been formed and, over the years, they had been cemented inside him as indisputable fact. In a way, not so different from her. She had embedded herself in the notion that safety was the top priority, because that was the lesson she had been taught growing up by her very protective father, and it was only when she had come to London to work and live that another reality had presented itself.

With Gabriel, he'd lived his life buried in the unemotional world of a high-octane work life with women as an enjoyment on the side-lines. He picked them up, he dropped them and they all seemed to blend into one another. Having worked alongside him for such a long time, she had long ago recognised the pattern.

Had the situation with Fifi changed something inside him? He'd pretty much said so himself. She had presented him with romance and an ultimatum, and he had ditched both at speed, but perhaps that had made him realise that he wasn't getting any younger and that settling down was really something he felt would work on some level.

And of course, having found family to embrace him, he had seen the other side of the coin when it came to marriage and family links.

He had glimpsed a middle road, a safe road where love wasn't a threat but companionship was a possibility—and here she was, fitting the bill. She was a known quantity. She was his efficient secretary who didn't make demands and always kept a cool head. She was also his lover now, and the sex was amazing.

So what if she'd told him that he wasn't her type? As it turned out, that was a lie, because he was very much her type and no doubt he'd sensed that. They were lovers and he knew just how much she wanted him. They wanted

one another and they got along and, without love to com-
plicate things, he had gravitated towards a proposal that
made sense for him.

But for her?

It had been hard enough doing what she was doing
now, having a sexual relationship with him while they
were here because she was in love and she was greedy
to make the most of him while she could. She knew that
once they were back in London she would have to start
looking for another job, because just facing him in the
office would be tough.

So, a life with him from which there was no exit plan;
being with him all the time, wanting more than he could
give and taking the crumbs that were offered; a life of
hiding how she really felt, knowing that to speak her feelings would be to risk it all: she couldn't begin to contemplate that.

'Gabriel, there must be a lot of other women out there
you could find to fill the role.'

'Stop being so unemotional about it,' he said, only part
in jest, just the slightest of frowns beginning.

'But isn't that what this is about?' she countered quietly. 'It would be a marriage, maybe not of convenience,
but a marriage without emotion.'

'There would be a lot of emotion...' He smiled slowly
and reached out to stroke her cheek, which made the
breath hitch in her throat. 'I can guarantee that.'

'Sex isn't an emotion, Gabriel.'

'I feel I can convince you that it is. Anyway, it's not
just the sex. It's the mutual respect we have for one another and the fact that we get along.'

'Thank you for the offer, but I'm afraid I'm going to
have to say no.'

'What?'

'I don't want to marry you.'

'Why? You don't mean that.' He raked his fingers through his hair. His frown had deepened; he was perplexed.

'I wouldn't say it if I didn't mean it.'

'Then explain.'

'Because,' she said flatly, 'I suppose I know what love feels like, and if I enter into another long-term relationship then I don't want to think that I'm sacrificing my chance to find it again in favour of practicality.'

She looked away from him because it was easier to be composed when she could ignore his dark eyes resting on her. 'I want the crazy declarations of love, Gabriel. Yes, sure, the sex is good between us—okay, the sex is great between us—and you like and respect me, which is nice, but in between those two things? That's what I want. I want the thing that's in between. I want to be the person the man I marry just can't live without. I want all the highs and the lows and the stormy arguments that bring us closer together. I want the excitement of planning babies together. I want all the passion that has nothing to do with sex, and that relationship—'

'Can't be with me.'

'It wouldn't work out, because it's not a case of box ticking.'

Gabriel sat back and gestured expressively and, when he next looked at her, his eyes were shuttered but he smiled.

'Fair enough.'

Fair enough? He'd just proposed, she'd turned him down and his response was *fair enough*?

Yet, why would it be anything else?

Gabriel knew what he was bringing to the table. He was stupidly rich, sinfully good-looking and, all in all, a catch. Yes, she might have made noises about just enjoying what they had while they were here—but on some instinctive level he would have sensed her weakness. And that would have wiped out any misgivings he might have had about what she wanted or how serious she was about wanting to end things once they returned to London.

The equation, for him, would have been easy. They liked one another, they respected one another, they were compatible and they were hot for one another. And, if he had decided that settling down with a woman might have some advantages, then he had simply gone and drawn conclusions that had suited him.

He was, after all, a guy who was very, very accustomed to getting what he wanted when it came to the opposite sex.

But it still hurt that he could abandon his pursuit with so little fight. For a couple of seconds, she wondered if, proposal rejected by Helen, he would make his next girlfriend a candidate for the role he now saw as vacant and desirable. Now that he had started thinking along the lines of marriage being advantageous, something achievable without real emotional investment, would his pattern of dating change? Would he stop the casual business of choosing women who were easy to walk away from? Would he now start interviewing for the one who would attach without making demands he would never be able to fulfil?

Marriage brought kids as well. From his interaction with Arturio and his various kids and grandchildren, he'd seen that there were up sides to family life, that making a fortune was meaningless if you had no one to spend any of it on.

Helen thought about working for him, and eventually having to see him get involved with someone on a serious level, and she quailed inside.

'So, let's put that aside.' She forced a smile while inside her heart twisted. 'And enjoy what's left of our holiday here. It's been such a great place—I've seen so many wonderful things.'

'Good.' His voice was clipped. 'Dinner awaits and then—I think I'll do some work. There's only so long a guy can play truant.'

Gabriel knew that it was stupid to be as unsettled as he was at her rejection.

He had never been rejected by a woman, but then he had never asked this question before. Was that it?

Replaying things in his head, he knew that he had somehow ended up making assumptions about her investment in what they'd shared.

What had made sense to him had stampeded through the reality that it wasn't a shared conclusion.

Marriage. Suddenly it had felt right for him to ask her. He'd seen family life at its best, thanks to Arturio and Isabella, and a series of events that he could never have predicted in a million years. And, even if he couldn't wholly embrace the business of love, even if his life lessons were just too deeply embedded, then he had realised how pointless it would be to die a billionaire with nothing left behind him in his wake.

He'd approached it from a practical point of view and because, like him, she was cool-headed and practical, he had assumed that his proposal would fall on fertile ground.

He was ashamed to think that any other woman would have bitten off his hand for a ring on her finger and all the vast benefits that came with that.

But she wasn't any other woman.

That said, he wasn't in the business of begging, but once he'd sat back and shrugged off her rejection he hadn't been able to face a night in bed with her.

It had grated on his nerves that she had been perfectly normal over an exquisite dinner he'd barely tasted. She'd smiled and chatted about the things she had enjoyed and, when that had petered out, she'd fallen back on the tried and tested work-related conversation.

He had no idea what she was thinking.

Now, back in London after a largely silent flight back from Italy, and after several days making do with a replacement because she had taken a few days to go visit her father, Gabriel sat at his desk, unable to focus on much, waiting for the door to his office to be pushed open… and only now realising how accustomed he had got to her presence.

It would be odd having her back, with all the water under the bridge, but it would be good, and things would settle right back into place: of that he had no doubt.

They always did for him. If he felt unsettled now, it was just because he was dealing with a situation that many had faced, just not him.

He relaxed back into his chair, his back to the floor-to-ceiling panes of glass that separated him from the busy streets several stories below. He didn't stand when he heard the knock on the door, but he did push back his chair, folded his arms and tilted his head to the side.

Familiarity warmed him. She was back in the office gear, the clothes that had been abandoned during their brief time out in Italy: navy skirt, white blouse, flat shoes and, he expected, a neat jacket tucked away on one of the hooks in her outer office.

Her hair was tied back and the golden glow of sun-kissed skin was fading. For a few seconds, he found that he couldn't quite say anything but, when he did, he dived right in with what was expected of him.

'Thanks for that report on the Turner deal,' he drawled, tilting back the chair and folding his hands behind his head. 'Really no need to have interrupted your holiday with work issues.'

He glanced at his computer, which was whirring, and then rested his dark eyes on her. Irritatingly, memory mingled with common sense, and he had to fight from his thoughts unravelling.

He tore his eyes away, frustrated with his own weakness, and gazed at the columns and numbers on his screen, aware of her slipping into the chair facing his desk, as she always did.

Helen had steeled herself for this.

What could she expect? At any rate, it was something she had to get over and done with, and she'd been was glad of the break to see her dad, which had gone a little way to easing the ball of nerves in the pit of her stomach.

She noted that he could barely meet her eyes. There had been no flash of—*anything*. He was already over it, and she knew that she shouldn't be surprised, because that was how it worked with him. She might occupy a different rank to the Fifis of this world but that didn't mean that she wasn't disposable, just like the rest of his girlfriends—marriage proposal or no marriage proposal.

But her heart was beating so fast, and she just wanted to drink him in, to succumb to the onslaught of sweet memories.

She slipped the letter out of her bag and shoved it across the desk to him.

'What's this?'

'You should read it.'

Once upon a long time ago, she had told him that she would hand in her notice if he couldn't obey her 'Keep Out' signs; if he couldn't accept that one kiss would never lead to anything more. So much water had flowed under that particular bridge and now it was truly impossible to pick up the working relationship they had left behind them. That was the conclusion she had reached during her stay in Cornwall, when she had done nothing but think and think and think.

She could stay on working for him, but there was no point kidding herself that seeing him every day, remembering what had happened between them and being exposed to his wit, charm and wonderful, mesmerising charisma wouldn't leave her a broken person.

She would have to leave; she would have to move on, take charge of her life and not let memories of him dictate a future of non-engagement. She didn't want to get buried under sadness and disillusionment. There were positives in life to be found even in the darkest of situations, and she would have to think that he had shown her what it felt like to be really and truly alive. And even if things had crashed and burned, that in itself was a blessing.

She had hung onto that silver lining during her week away and made the most of it. She had phoned the one friend she knew who could yank her out of the doldrums and arranged to meet as soon as she was back in London. If she had to get back on the bike, the sooner she got on, the better and Lucy, who knew her better than anyone, would help with that.

She had been *proactive*.

Their eyes met and he slowly took the piece of paper, read what was written on it and pushed it to one side.

'No.'

'No what?'

'No, I don't accept your resignation.'

'You can't *not* accept my resignation, Gabriel.'

'This wasn't part of the plan!'

'Plans change.' She jutted her chin at a defiant angle and stared at him for a few seconds. 'I did some thinking when I went to see my dad and I realised that, after everything that's happened between us, working closely with you would be impossible for me.'

'Why?'

He pushed himself aggressively away from his desk and walked jerkily towards the bank of windows, leaning against one of the glass panes to glare at her.

With the sun streaming behind him, he was a towering, imposing silhouette—a dominant alpha male reacting to something he didn't like.

'Why do you think?'

'We agreed that we would only embark on—what we embarked on—on the understanding that it wouldn't affect our working relationship.' He knew—of course he did. Having always been the guy who did nothing without first working out possible consequences—the guy who knew how to control life, because it was better he control life than life control him—he had thrown it all through the window and galloped down a road that had led him right to this point.

'Maybe I can't be as unemotional about it as you, Gabriel.'

'What are you trying to say?'

His dark eyes skewered her with focused concentration.

Helen breathed in deeply and met that unwavering stare with equal coolness.

She remembered his mouth on hers, his hands touching her, his head buried between her legs, and a shiver of powerful awareness raced through her.

'Are you trying to tell me that…'

'I'm trying to tell you that life would be easier for me if I didn't have to work with you on a daily basis. I thought I could. I can't. Too much water under the bridge. It would be uncomfortable and awkward, and I wouldn't be able to get around that, and there's no reason why I should try. There's a thriving job market out there and I think I would be able to find a job without too much difficulty. Provided, that is, I get a good reference from you.'

'*Provided you get a good reference from me?* Who do you think I am, Helen? I really thought we knew each other better than that—better than for you to think that I could ever be the sort of person vengeful and spiteful enough to somehow make you pay for walking out on me.'

Helen flushed. 'I'm not *walking out on you*, Gabriel.'

'That's *exactly* what you're doing!' He shrugged elaborately. 'But, if that's the road you want to go down, then so be it. You will leave my employ with an impeccable reference, which is no less than you deserve.'

'Thank you.' She hesitated. 'You don't understand…'

'Really?'

'It's more than just the fact that things would be awkward between us.' She was thinking on her feet. 'For me, at any rate.' To leave with her dignity intact felt very important. 'Maybe that proposal of yours made me think— just as it probably made *you* think.'

'I'm not following you.' But a dark flush highlighted his cheekbones as he met her gaze with narrow-eyed, scowling intensity.

'Maybe,' Helen said slowly, 'it made me think that it really is time for me to get back into the dating scene.'

'The *dating scene*?'

'Yes, Gabriel.'

'The Internet is full of losers and men on the lookout for vulnerable women.'

'I think I'm grown up enough to handle myself. Besides…'

'Besides what?'

'Besides…' She was protecting herself, forcing him to see her not just as another of his women who would leave with a broken heart, despite her protestations to the contrary, but as her own woman capable of looking out for herself. 'There are other places to meet people. My friend Lucy is great fun and we're already planning evenings out. It's been a while coming.' It was not a lie; vague plans had been made. Saying it out loud though, felt committal. Like it or not, a future of moving on was taking shape at the speed of light.

'Evenings out? Where?'

Helen wondered what was so shocking about what she'd just said—nothing. Yet, judging from his tone of voice, anyone would think that she'd just told him that she'd signed up for a career in pole dancing.

Did he think that she was incapable of braving the big, bad world out there? Perhaps he figured that he knew her well enough to suspect that *evenings out* in search of a suitable partner would be way beyond her remit?

If she was honest, he had a point, but she had embarked on this line of self-defence, so she would just have to see it through.

'Bars. Pubs. Clubs.' It was nerve-racking just thinking about it.

'Bars? Pubs? Clubs?'

'It's not beyond the pale, Gabriel. I'm young. It's what girls of my age do.'

'You're not a bar, pub or club person, damn it!'

'You don't know what sort of person I am!'

'We both know that's a lie.'

'Why would it matter to you one way or another if Lucy and I decide to go bar-hopping?' From vague plans to imminent bar-hopping. She had never bar-hopped in her life before. She had never pub-crawled. Her one time at a club had involved a broken heel of her brand-new high-heeled shoes.

'It doesn't,' Gabriel ground out forcefully.

The thought of her going from bar to bar, getting more and more intoxicated, made him feel sick. She barely drank. In his head, he had images of her being pursued by drunken strangers, misreading signals she wasn't sending out because she just wasn't a 'bar' person. He had no idea who this Lucy character was, but he assumed someone happy to lead someone else off the straight and narrow, even if that someone else was supposedly a friend.

Of course, what she did henceforth was none of his business, but was it any surprise that he was inclined to feel a certain amount of protectiveness towards her?

This wasn't just one of those women he dated who was experienced in the ways of the world.

'Good,' Helen murmured, looking down at her entwined fingers. 'And, just for the record, I have quite some holiday stored up, so I'm entitled to take it in lieu of working my notice.'

'This is crazy! You're acting as though…'

'As though…?'

'As though we're not friends,' Gabriel muttered with biting incredulity.

Helen whitened. In a nutshell he had found the core of her unhappiness and dragged it out into the open.

This man was more than just a guy she had fallen into bed with against all better judgement. This man was her friend, and the thought of walking out of these offices never to see him again was unbearable.

For a second, she wondered what would happen if she'd accepted his crazy proposal, but she reminded herself that storing up heartbreak was no way to spend her life. And, besides, it was a moot point because no sooner had that proposal been made than she had swiftly rejected it.

'I don't want you to think that,' she said gruffly. 'Of course we're friends. If you—really want me to stay and work out my notice, then I will.'

Gabriel waved his hand dismissively. 'Not important. You want to go? I wouldn't dream of standing in your way.' He moved abruptly towards her, towering over her, before reaching down, hands planted on either side of her chair, caging her in so that she could scarcely breathe for want of his proximity. 'But as your friend and, believe it or not, someone who cares about you, I would like to offer a word of warning.'

Helen didn't really want to hear about him caring about her because it was so far removed from the crazy passion she felt for him. They'd been lovers, but now that was off the cards and what remained for him was friendship.

Who wanted to be buddies with a guy they were in love with? That line of thinking gave her some much-needed backbone, powering her to withstand his chummy, patronising advice.

'What's that?'

'Pace yourself with the drinking and don't hand out your phone number to anyone, however convincing he might seem.'

Helen's eyebrows shot up and she offered him a wry smile. 'Repeat—I think I'll be okay out there in the big, bad world and, besides, I'll be with Lucy, my closest friend.'

Gabriel frowned.

'Mind me asking when this drinking session in bars and clubs is going to get under way?'

'Gabriel, I don't need your guiding hand when it comes to my social life,' Helen told him, but there was a slow heat burning a path through her and she wished he would just stand up so that she could get her breathing back under control. 'And, as for when we're going to have a night out, who knows? Maybe Friday. Everyone goes out on a Friday.'

There was no room for daydreaming. She knew that if she did that she would stagnate and the years would creep up on her while she busied herself thinking about the past. She might as well get her head around one or two concrete plans.

It was agreed that she would work to the end of the week. Julie, who filled in occasionally in Helen's absence, would temporarily hold the fort but would have to be shown the ropes.

'I'll leave it to you,' Gabriel said, stalking back to his desk and killing the personal and awkward conversation they had been having. 'I have several meetings that will take me out of London, so don't expect me to be around much.'

Helen smiled, annoyed with herself for not wanting that personal conversation to end; annoyed with herself for thinking that it showed protectiveness towards her, perhaps even *possessiveness*, and baulking at the commitment she had made to herself that Friday would be the start of a new chapter in her life. She didn't quite feel ready for new chapters just yet.

'Great.' She shot him a brittle, mega-watt smile and told herself that not having him around was going to do wonders for her nervous system.

Gabriel made it to the office a little after six on the Friday evening.

It was still way too hot and way too sunny. He'd just sat through a five-hour meeting and, even with the top two buttons of his shirt undone, he still felt uncomfortable. The crush of people on the streets threading their way through the city had got on his nerves.

Why was London always so busy? It had made him think of Genoa, the vineyards and a way of life that was calm, laid back and unstressed. At least, comparatively. The days there had melded into one another and the nights had been filled with making love.

Why couldn't she see what he did in the idea of a union that could work?

He clenched his jaw in raw frustration. His week had

been hellish. True to his word, he had disappeared from his office, leaving Helen to work out the last remaining days of her notice, showing Julie the ropes.

Had he actually been able to concentrate, however? No. He'd found himself sitting in on high-level meetings, his mind a thousand miles away, contributing to proceedings without his usual incisive rigour.

Another woman, maybe? A return to his usual pattern of behaviour?

The thought of seeing someone else, of even getting in touch with another woman, had been enough to make him feel reasonably sick.

Truth was, *he missed her.*

He missed everything about her. He couldn't bear the thought of spending any amount of time in his office because he couldn't face her. And, somewhere along the line, he remembered what he had said when they had first embarked on their charade. She had asked him how Arturio would believe that a guy like him had fallen for his secretary, and he had mused that it was very credible that he had found that what he wanted had been right there all along—the woman who knew him better than anyone ever had.

How stupid and blind he'd been not to see the truth behind that throwaway remark.

He'd had the most precious thing in the world for a moment in time and he had thrown away the chance to show her that he... *That he loved her.* He'd been so securely locked up in his ivory tower, and so convinced that nothing and no one could make a dent in it, that he hadn't realised that this wonderful woman had entered through the front door and set up camp in his heart.

How could he not have guessed? Looking back, he'd

treated her completely differently from every other woman he'd ever dated. He'd talked to her, opened up, revealed weaknesses without even realising; and, if he'd realised, he airbrushed over any discomfort at it.

He'd trusted her with his heart, whether he'd known it at the time or not. She hadn't seen it and he'd been too obtuse to point it out.

And now it was too late.

He thought about her hitting the singles scene and wanted to see the bottom of a whisky bottle to deal with the pain.

And, just like that, thoughts all over the place and barely aware of his surroundings as he pushed open the glass doors to the building in which his offices were housed, he saw her...

CHAPTER TEN

His breathing quickened. She was in a pale-blue dress that was a couple of inches above her knees, had flung a silky cardigan over her shoulders and was wearing white trainers. The whole ensemble was quirky, cute and ridiculously sexy and he stopped dead in his tracks and just stared.

In the periphery of his vision, he made out her companion, a small, curvy blonde with curly hair who was wearing something or other. He barely noticed because his eyes were all for Helen who, after a moment's surprised hesitation, was now looking back at him with an expression he couldn't read.

She walked towards him and made polite introductions.

Lucy—the blonde companion intent on leading her astray although, in fairness, the blonde companion didn't look like someone inclined to lead anyone astray. Who knew, though?

'Apologies I haven't seen much of you this week,' he opened gruffly. 'But thank for keeping me updated on the transfer over of duties.'

Helen produced a tight smile. 'No problem. I think Julie is going to work out very well in the short term, although she's made it clear that she doesn't want a permanent transfer, as she's very loyal to Simon.' She turned to Lucy,

whose blue eyes were darting between them with interest. 'Remember I told you that I'm leaving the company?'

'So you did. Bye-bye to the old and hello to the new.'

'So it would seem,' Gabriel remarked tersely, settling
his gaze on the blonde as he detected something that
sounded a little like wicked amusement in her remark. Or
maybe she was just stirring the pot. 'Which clubs are you
two going to target?' he asked with a lot of fake bonhomie.

His eyes were back on Helen. His mind was still playing with the realisation that he had fallen in love with her.
Thinking about her deprived him of the ability to speak,
it would seem, because she answered and he barely took
in what she had said.

He was remembering how she'd looked after they'd
made love, the flush on her cheeks, the drowsy darkness
of her eyes, the soft curve of her body against his.

Conversations had been had, low and murmured, and
he could kick himself now for never having worked out the
significance of them—never having realised that, bit by
bit, those conversations had changed the man he had been
into a man he had never thought himself capable of being.
Having spent his life vacating the bed as soon as the hot
business of making love was done, he had found himself
lingering between the sheets, warm, lazy and happy to
talk with her curled into him, his hand stroking her hair.

The significance of that had foolishly passed him by.

'I… There are always any of the clubs I belong to.' He
raked his fingers through his hair and forced a smile. 'You
know which they are, Helen.'

'Indeed I do. I've made arrangements for several din-
ners there for you and one of your many Fifis.'

'Use my name. Don't pay for anything. You can put
whatever you want on my tab. You've worked for me for

years and—I would like to spare no expense on your evening out. I… Yes, well, whatever you want—lobster and caviar, champagne. Money's no object.'

'Thank you very much. It's a kind offer but I'm sure we'll find somewhere nice enough and not too expensive. Won't we, Luce?'

'Sure will.'

Gabriel dragged his eyes away from Helen to focus on the small blonde next to her. He could see curiosity and amusement there, and he frowned.

'I know a couple of good places,' she said, glancing down but still smiling. 'Great places for two girls out to have some fun. I've been after Helen to get out there with me and for us to enjoy ourselves.' She dimpled and Gabriel's frown deepened.

'Is that what you want, Helen?' he asked brusquely.

'Course it is,' Lucy said airily. 'Isn't it, Helen? Loud music, guys buying us drinks, dancing round our handbags…'

'Yep.' Helen stared straight into Gabriel's cool, dark, disapproving eyes with defiance.

Was he going to give her another lecture on how to look after herself? Where would *he* be going later, anyway? He wasn't a 'Friday night is stay-at-home-night' kind of guy. He was more a 'where's my little black book and which gorgeous blonde shall I call? Because it's Friday, after all…' kind of guy.

Although, he looked tired. Haggard, even.

'Helen…' His voice was a little jagged. Why was he bothering to play the part of the guy who didn't care? He cared. He more than cared. If he hadn't bumped into her here, then he knew that he would have done what he intended to do now—he would have found her and begged for her time, flung himself at her mercy.

She'd said that she wanted the stuff that came along with the passion and the friendship, the stuff that made a relationship worth its salt—the stuff called *love*.

The very thing he'd removed from the table when he had asked her to marry him.

It was time to vacate his ivory tower.

'Gabriel, we should be heading off now.'

'Can we…talk?'

'Haven't we already?'

'Please.' He heard some soft laughter from the blonde with the smart mouth, but he couldn't get annoyed, because every scrap of his attention was focused on the woman she was with.

Helen hesitated. Gabriel was a guy who never begged. She'd never thought he had the vocabulary for it, and certainly not the disposition. But there was a pleading in his voice that made her breathing hitch and, looking at him more closely, she could see that he really did look haggard.

There was wickedness in Lucy's voice, next to her, as she murmured something about leaving them to it, that the pub wasn't going to go anywhere any time soon.

'Don't be silly,' Helen said a little weakly.

Were those new lines by his mouth? she wondered. Why did he look haggard? Was she being over-imaginative? Reading things into something that was straightforward? She thought of those times when she had seen him shorn of his usual self-assurance. He looked like that now: human; vulnerable; uncertain. And absolutely adorable.

When she next glanced away, it was to see her friend backing away and waving goodbye. And was that a wink…?

'Who *is* that woman?' He said this to buy a little time now that he was alone with Helen. He raked his fingers through his hair and was aware of a level of nervous tension he just wasn't used to.

'My closest friend. I should join her.' Considering Lucy had disappeared, and Helen's feet were glued to the ground, this felt like an empty statement.

'Please don't. Please stay, hear me out. Please,' Gabriel said gruffly.

He was going to do it. He was going to do the one thing he never dreamed possible. He was going to spill his soul.

The love he felt for this woman was too heavy to carry around for ever without letting her know.

'I'm crazy about you.'

There. Why beat about the bush? He flushed darkly but he didn't look away.

Helen opened her mouth and stared at Gabriel. She wanted to shake those words out of her head because she didn't want them to carry her away on some stupid, hopeful, falsely optimistic journey.

'I know a wine bar just round the corner,' he continued urgently into the silence.

'Gabriel, we've done all the talking we need to do. I've told you how I feel.' Her protest sounded weak even to her own ears.

'But I am yet to tell you how *I* feel.'

He circled her arm and gently began ushering her out of the towering glass skyscraper.

It was busy, with people everywhere, inside the building and outside.

'Please, Helen,' he said quietly, although she hadn't protested. He dropped her arm and stood back, giving her the chance to blow him off and she wondered what he would do, how he would persuade her to hear him out, if she did.

Surely he couldn't blame her for her reluctance. How could he? He'd made sure to bang on about being unavailable, handing her so many warning notices that she could have papered a room with them. On top of that, she knew his form. Knew him inside out.

'Okay, but then I'm going to meet Lucy.'

'Thank you.'

He was crazy about her? She wanted to ask him to clarify but she wasn't going to.

They walked briskly round the corner to a wine bar that was brimming with people, full inside and with clusters of after-work groups hanging around outside, drinks in hand, relaxing after a week at it. The thought of joining them as she resumed life as a single ready to mingle was daunting.

They found a seat, which came as no surprise, because he was the sort of guy who *found seats*.

'Well?' They were both sitting with two glasses of wine in front of them. Helen looked at him and her heart skipped a beat. It hadn't been the same, being at the office without him there, knowing that she was saying goodbye to what had been a huge part of her life for years. She'd been giddy with misery and exhausted from having to put a smile on her face so that Julie didn't expect anything.

She'd managed to vaguely say something about having to quit because of personal problems, and it had been left there. To look as miserable as she'd felt would have courted the sort of quiet curiosity she hadn't thought she could bear.

'Well, I've done a lot of thinking, Helen. The past week has been...' He shook his head and raked his fingers through his hair in a gesture of wearied frustration. 'A mess for me.'

Helen lowered her eyes, blocked her mind from playing fanciful games and made an effort to stick to the programme.

'I'm sorry about the lack of notice. I wouldn't have done it if I hadn't thought that it would be for the best.'

'Naturally.'

'I may have dealt with a broken engagement but I'd had the chance to leave, to make sure I put some distance between me and George. But to continue working for you after everything that happened? It wouldn't have been the sort of comfortable working environment I could have dealt with. And then, you would have picked up where you left off with other women... No, that's not something I felt I had to put up with.'

'I admit I've—not been exemplary when it comes to longevity and women,' Gabriel admitted heavily.

'That's the understatement of the year.' She gulped down some wine and tried not to wince at the size of the mouthful. 'It's not just that...' She sighed, fiddled with the stem of the glass and realised that, although there was noise all around them, the buzz of people laughing and talking, they seemed to be caught in a little silent bubble of their own.

'That...what?'

'It's not just that you haven't had longevity with any

of the women you've dated. It's the fact that you're just not interested in having a serious, committed relationship with anyone. It's not a case that no woman has come along who captured your imagination. You haven't been looking for love and failing to find it. You're just not interested in looking at all.'

'You know my back story.'

'I know your childhood was an unhappy one, Gabriel.' She looked at him with empathetic, serious eyes which were nevertheless unflinching. 'If you've chosen to let that determine all the choices you make when it comes to involvement with someone else, then that's your business. I've had my fair share of learning curves as well, but in the end life goes on.'

'Yes, it does, and I've finally seen that.'

'What do you mean?'

When she looked at her glass, she was surprised to see that it was empty. She couldn't remember gulping down more wine but she must have done. He topped up her glass and she didn't stop him. There was nothing wrong with a little Dutch courage.

'You're right,' Gabriel said simply. 'I've always let my past determine my present and my future. My parents were absent, so wrapped up in themselves and in the business of having fun that there was never any real point of reference for me growing up. They seldom made it to parents' meetings when I was at boarding school. They never bothered with sports days. They couldn't. They were usually not in the country and it never occurred to them to make an effort to try to be. At the end of each term, I was collected by one of the staff, ferried to a private jet and taken wherever it was arranged I should go and, during the holidays, they might or might not have popped in.'

'I know. I feel so sorry for you. Money really doesn't buy everything, does it?'

Gabriel smiled with bitter irony. 'No, my darling, it doesn't. And yet for a long time I deluded myself into thinking that the only things I wanted were the things it could buy. It was my default position. There was safety in things that were tangible—in houses and cars and boats. Emotions? Love? Those were the things that caused pain and damage, and so those were the things to be avoided at all costs.'

'You're not telling me anything I didn't already know, Gabriel.'

Had he actually called her 'darling'? Or had her fevered mind played tricks on her?

'Here's what you don't know. You don't know how things changed for me. You don't know that I ripped up the road map I'd spent my life following without even realising it. You don't know how it was that you came into my life and nothing was the same for me again.'

Helen's eyes widened and she tilted her head to one side, her expression silently questioning what he had just said.

Gabriel shrugged. 'I know. You don't believe me, and I don't blame you. I've been a fool, Helen. I don't know how else to put it. I never realised that over the years I became more and more embedded in you.

'You were the constant in my life. I thought I was standing still but, in fact, you were changing my direction and it all came to a head when we—when we went to America and the protective walls of the office were removed. I don't know if things would have changed for me, had we remained in London, had life carried on its same trajectory with you coming in, doing a great job at work and leaving the office—never letting me in. I think that eventually we would have ended up in the same place.'

'That's assuming I felt the same way, which is a pretty sweeping assumption.' Her words were firm, her voice was not.

'Did you?'

'I...'

'This is a time for us to be completely honest with one another, Helen. I—I'm not the sort of guy who does this emotional stuff, but I couldn't function this past week. Nothing made sense and nothing mattered. You were going, and I was broken up, because somehow I've managed to fall madly in love with you. The thought of never seeing you again is a thought that...'

He shook his head and briefly looked away, but his jaw clenched and his fingers tightened around the stem of his wine glass. He looked back at her. 'So...did you? Feel the same? Feel that we were both attracted to one another over the time we've worked together? That what happened between us in America was somehow inevitable?'

'Actually, *attraction* doesn't begin to cover it. Not for me, even though that was the deal I wanted to kid myself was going on with you. No, for me, it would be more truthful to say that you became embedded in my soul, and the physical attraction that finally exploded between us was just a symptom of something a lot bigger that was going on underneath.'

'You—*you're in love with me*?'

Her heart skipped several beats. Was he telling the truth? His voice was raw with sincere emotion and yet it seemed unbelievable. But surely he wouldn't make something like that up because she'd rejected him and he wanted to have her back in his bed, whatever it took? Because he couldn't take no for an answer?

He'd said that this was a time for them to be honest with one another.

'If you were that crazy about me, then why didn't you say anything sooner?' she asked bluntly.

'Because, like I said, I didn't know how. I didn't have the words. I made assumptions about myself and believed them to be true, even when all my actions and all my thoughts were telling me that I'd changed.'

'I want to believe you, I really do,' she whispered, tentatively letting go of some of her suspicions as her heart opened up to what he was saying.

'Because?'

'Because…' she breathed in deeply '…because I feel the same way about you.'

There was a thickening silence. Gabriel reached out to link her fingers in his and his spirits soared when she didn't yank her hand away.

'But you turned down my marriage proposal!'

'Because I needed more than just a ring on my finger and good sex and compatibility. I needed more than just a business arrangement.'

'And you're ready to move on with me?' Gabriel asked quietly. 'No regrets down the road about taking the plunge and handing your heart over to the guy who always swore he'd never release his into anyone's safe-keeping until now?'

'None,' Helen said with complete honesty. 'You know, I always believed in love. Dad went to pieces after Mum and my brother died, and he never met anyone again, but I was never scared of giving my heart away just because I knew that loving someone could lead to hurt. I thought I was safe with you because you weren't the sort of guy who would ever be on my radar, but I fell in love, and when I did I knew it had to be all or nothing with you, not a road in between. I love you, Gabriel, and I always will.'

'Then,' he said roughly, 'At the risk of being repetitive, will you marry me?'

Helen smiled and touched his cheek with her finger.

'Just try and stop me.'

The wedding was a small affair. Neither wanted to hang around, planning anything over the top, although the option was offered.

'Not me,' Helen had said. 'Not my style.'

She wore a cream silk dress that cinched in at the waist and fell in soft layers to mid-calf, and her hair was piled up and threaded with tiny flowers that matched the bouquet she carried.

Gabriel turned around, saw her as she walked up the aisle in the tiny local church where she had grown up in Cornwall and his heart had clenched with love.

He'd finally given himself permission to love and not a minute went past when he didn't thank everything there was to thank that she was a part of his life.

He smiled, and when he cast his eyes over the congregation he felt a sense of satisfaction at the warmth and the love radiating from it.

He saw her father and her friends—including Lucy, who had told him what a lucky guy he was to have nabbed her best friend, a sentiment with which he couldn't disagree. And his friends, some from his days at university, and a couple from boarding school, all forming a tightly knit group in his life.

And of course Arturio and Isabella, who could not have been more delighted with the outcome.

And now…

Gabriel glanced over to where his wife was sitting, feet resting on an upholstered pouffe, television on in the little snug of the cottage they had bought on the outskirts of London—close enough for him to get the train into the City as and when, but far enough out that there was land and fields around them.

There was also ample room for visitors and her father had already visited several times since they had moved in.

'Anything?' he asked, nudging her feet a couple of inches with his and looking at her with love.

'Trust me, you'll be the first to know the very second I feel any twinges.' She glanced at her very pregnant belly and smiled at him. 'I'm only four days overdue. I could be another week. Who knows? Although…' she rolled her eyes '…I can't wait. I feel like a beached whale most of the time.'

'I can't wait either,' Gabriel confided in a husky undertone.

'You might not be saying that when your nights start getting interrupted with a mini-me yelling for milk.'

'Bring it on.' He grinned and rubbed his knuckle across her cheek. 'I can't wait to meet this baby we've made, my darling, and to carry on with this fantastic new chapter in my life.'

Helen smiled back and rested her hand on her belly. 'Nor,' she sighed happily, 'can I.'

* * * * *

If A Wedding Negotiation with Her Boss
left you wanting more,
then look out for the next instalment in the
Secrets of Billionaire's Secretaries duet,
coming soon!

And in the meantime,
why not dive into these other stories
by Cathy Williams?

A Week with the Forbidden Greek
The Housekeeper's Invitation to Italy
The Italian's Innocent Cinderella
Unveiled as the Italian's Bride
Bound by Her Baby Revelation

Available now!